CASTAWAY
AND OTHER
TALES FROM MAURITIUS

by

RAMESH RAMDOYAL

To
All Islanders
Young and Old
and
All Island Lovers

Acknowledgements

Rama Poonoosamy, who through his *Collection Maurice*, encouraged me and others to write;
Jonah Peerally for sharing his story with me;
Chic and Shobha Fulena, Meera, and other friends who shared their experiences with me;
Sachita Ramdin for formatting and preparing Createspace and Kindle ready copies of this book, and for the cover layouts;
The Raphael Fishing Co. Ltd for photos of Raphael Island;
George Hughes: *Between the Tides: In Search of Sea Turtles*;
The Proceedings of the Royal Society of Arts and Sciences of Mauritius, 1968.
Loretta de Plevitz: *Restless Energy: A Biography of Adolphe de Plevitz.*
St John of the Cross: *The Spiritual Canticle.*

Table of Contents

CASTAWAY

Xavier and his son, Manuel, had set out early in the morning in search of big fish. They put out four lines - two baited with live sardines trailing about 150 ft for smaller fish, and two heavy lines baited with live bonito trailing about 250 ft for big marlin.

They had gone far out in their pirogue and could hardly see the grey-green line of the shore or the tops of the grey-blue mountains that rose above the land. But that didn't make any difference. Xavier could bring a boat in at any time of the day or night by the alignment of the mountains against landmarks on the shore.

By five p.m., they had caught two small dorados and three medium-sized tunas. But they hadn't set out to catch 'small' fish. The big-game fishing season was almost over and they hadn't yet caught a single marlin to cheer their hearts during the long lean winter months ahead. They had gone out that day praying secretly it was going to be their lucky day.

The sun was dipping low on the horizon and soon it was going to be swallowed up by the sea. Just then Xavier sighted a large flock of birds circling and swirling in the distance.

'They're following a big shoal,' Xavier thought to himself. 'And judging by the presence of *pailles-en-queues*, some big fish must be around!'

Xavier turned on his small outboard motor at full throttle and raced after the flock.

'The birds are a big help,' Xavier told Manuel, 'they see the small fish from a great height and chase after them to feed themselves. The big fish chase after the small fish for their food.

We can't see the fish in the water but we can see the birds in the sky from far away. We therefore follow the birds to catch the big fish that chase after the small fish!'

Just then Xavier felt a pull on one of the lines that lay under his feet. Catching hold of the line, he let it slip through his fingers as something very heavy started moving away with the bait.

'Eat the bonito, fish. It tastes good, doesn't it?' he chuckled aloud. He held the line loose to let the fish swallow the bait completely. He then jerked the line with both his hands to let the hook bite deeply into the fish's guts. Then he pulled and pulled with all the strength of his arms. But he didn't gain a single inch of line. On the contrary, the line started to hiss and run, uncoiling the pile of cord that he had kept in reserve.

'Manuel!' he shouted, 'there's a big one on my line. Pull all the other lines in. They must not get in the way. Cut off the baited hooks. Tie all the lines end to end to give us as much reserve line as possible to play the fish!'

The big fish started to move away and the line kept hissing and running. The speed of the line was burning and cutting Xavier's hands.

'Quick, pour seawater on the coil to keep the lines wet!' Xavier shouted.

The line went out and out and out. Unless checked, the fish was going to run away with all the line.

'Tie the free end of the line to the thwart!' he shouted.

When all the line had been played out, the pirogue began to be pulled far out.

The sun had long sunk beneath the horizon and the night was pitch dark. The fish kept moving in a north-north easterly direction farther and farther away from the island with the pirogue in tow.

2

When the day broke the land was no longer visible. The sea stretched endlessly in all directions. The hours passed. The fish kept pulling the boat away.

Night fell but the fish showed no sign of tiring.

Xavier could cut the fish loose and return to shore. But he didn't have the heart to cut the line. He decided he was going to fight the fish to the finish.

'This is it fish. It's either you or me!' he muttered through clenched teeth.

Passing the line over his shoulder and across his back, he held it firm with both hands and started pulling with all the strength of his arms and body. Just then the fish broke through the water, leaping and twisting and falling back with a big splash. Again and again the mighty fish jumped and twisted on his tail as he tried to break free of the cruel iron hook that was killing him.

Xavier was feeling faint and sick, and his eyes were burning with the sun and the salt in them.

He could feel the fish weakening and the line slackening. He wrapped the line around his body and tried to get the fish alongside the boat. But just when he thought he had succeeded, the fish leapt away shattering the thwart to which the line was fastened, dragging Xavier overboard to his death.

In a desperate attempt to stop the drift of the boat, Manuel cast the anchor overboard and paddled against the current. But it was no use. The current was far too strong and the boat was swept farther and farther out. When he was completely exhausted, Manuel crouched in a corner of the boat and cried until he fell asleep.

When he woke up in the morning, no land was visible anywhere. He was all alone in the middle of a vast ocean.

3

Manuel was feeling very hungry and thirsty. He ate the rest of the bread that was left and drained the few drops of water that remained in the gallon they had brought. Before the sun went down, Manuel chewed the raw flesh of the fish they had caught. On the fourth day all the water had run out and the remaining fish had begun to stink and had to be thrown overboard. Fortunately It rained that night and Manuel could slake his thirst with the rainwater that had collected at the bottom of the boat.

By the next morning, Manuel could see dozens of flying fish, no bigger than herrings, breaking from the water and shooting across the bows of the boat to fall into the sea a few yards away. A few of them, much to Manuel's relief, fell into the boat. 'They're good for eating,' Manuel thought as he forced a few bits and pieces down his throat and saved the rest of the fish for later. There was nothing to do but shelter himself from the scorching sun and try not to feel too miserable.

By nightfall Manuel was feeling nauseous and weak. He lay down and tried to sleep. But each time he began to fall asleep, he was kept awake by spray on his face or by squalls of rain. When he woke up in the morning, he could see in the distance a few birds skimming the surface of the sea and he knew that land could not be very far away. An hour later, he could make out far down on the western horizon a long line of reef encircling a vast lagoon. As he drew closer, he started paddling vigorously towards a low-lying part of the reef over which the rollers were breaking evenly. When he was only a few yards away, his boat was caught in a swell and swept over the reef into the lagoon. He was projected violently and nearly drowned after his boat hit a clump of coral. When he came to the surface, he was carried by the incoming tide and washed on the beach badly bruised

4

and battered. The last thing he remembered before passing out was the figure of a man armed with an axe approaching him.

THE FUGITIVE

Manuel's crash-landing had not gone unnoticed. A pair of eyes had been closely watching the boat's every move ever since it had come within sight of the island. The eyes belonged to Xara, a fugitive from justice who had been shipwrecked on the island some three years back.

Xara came from the island of Mauritius, and used to contract out his services for six to twelve months at a time to work on the boats that fished the distant shoals and sandbanks around Saint Brandon, Agalega and the Chagos archipelago.

One night, unknown to his wife, he had returned home unexpectedly and found his wife on the couch with his best friend. Mad with rage, Xara had stabbed his wife and her 'lover' to death. He had then travelled to Port Louis and embarked on a boat bound for the distant banks on a long fishing expedition. The boat had later been caught in a storm and wrecked on the reef encircling the islands of the Saint Brandon archipelago.

The ship, the *Tropic Bird*, was a total wreck. Her back was broken and she lay wedged sidelong on the reef where the surf would batter her to pieces. All the occupants on board had drowned. Xara was the only survivor.

He had been able to swim to one of the islands in the lagoon. His arrival on the atoll was greeted by the squeaks and squawks from thousands of seabirds that nested in the sparse vegetation lining the beach.

Then he scoured the beach to pick up anything that's been washed overboard - broken spars and planking, cans and wooden crates.

5

After a few days, the boat was sucked back into the big deep during a high sea. There remained not a sign of a shipwreck. Xara knew that search parties would be sent out for a while, and then along with the rest of the crew, he would be reported dead or missing.

Xara then explored the island and found it to be densely populated by birds, mostly albatross and *ye-ye* (sooty terns) and covered in many places by a thick carpet of guano. The land abounded in birds' eggs and was sparsely covered with bushes, thickets and a few coconut palms.

The lagoon swarmed with fish. Fast green turtles chased each other in the crystal-clear water and came to lay their eggs in places shielded from the birds.

He found a few abandoned corrugated iron shacks that must have been used by fishermen in the past to store the fish they had caught and to prepare them for shipment. He also found a big cave and decided to hide away there. He could easily camouflage the entrance in case stray fishermen landed on the island.

Months passed and no one came. After ascertaining that the island was completely deserted and no longer used, he decided to live there for as long as it was necessary, safe from the police and outside the reach of the law.

The last thing he wanted was visitors.

When Xara saw Manuel's boat swept over the reef and the boy washed on the beach, he rushed out with his axe, determined to eliminate anyone who could be a threat to his security.

Manuel's body was lying inert on the beach. His limbs had been gashed and lacerated by sharp coral, and unless treated quickly, the infection from the wounds was going to poison his bloodstream and spread all over his body. Xara could walk away and leave the boy to die. And that would have been the end of it. But when he looked at the boy's face, he was moved by a feeling of tenderness he hadn't felt for a very long time. The boy looked so helpless, so innocent. He was too young to die. Xara quickly pumped the water from his body, heaved him on to his shoulders and hurried to his hideout. He laid him down on a bed of dried leaves and bathed his wounds with rainwater that he kept in large clams. He then rubbed in some crab-oil and a paste made from plants that grew on the island. He then wrapped his limbs in bandages of cool leaves.

When Manuel opened his eyes, he was scared and shouted for his mother.
'Don't be afraid,' Xara reassured him and patted him gently. 'You are in safe hands. I'm going to look after you. Now I'm going to fix you a meal. Eat it all to get back your strength.'

When Manuel had recovered completely, Xara taught him how to make a fire by focusing the rays of the sun through a lens on a pile of dry grass, leaves, twigs and bits of dry bark. Xara taught Manuel how to dig wells and collect rainwater in clam shells and coconut cups. He showed him how and when to collect fresh birds' eggs and trap sea turtles that came to lay their eggs.
He taught him how to fish with lines made from coconut fibres and hooks made of shells. He taught him how to weave fish-traps and bake fish in a wrapping of leaves in a fire-pit over hot stones.
From time to time when they were in the mood, they would light a fire on the beach and pile on dead branches till they had a

roaring fire going. They would grill fish and turtle eggs and have a feast. They would sit by the fire and talk, sing and tell stories until late in the night. More often than not, their celebration ended with reminiscences of Mauritius.

'Do you know what I miss most apart from my family,' Manuel told Xara one day, 'I miss the good time I had with my friends over the weekends. We sat around a fire on the beach and sang and danced. I played the guitar and my brother Patrice played the *ravann*. Tourists left their big five-star hotels and sang and danced with us. My dad told us: "We don't need to live in five-star hotels. Look at the sky full of stars, we live in a million-star hotel !" '

'I understand how you feel, Manuel,' Xara said. 'Many Mauritians do not think much of their country. It is only when they leave Mauritius that they realise how much it means to them (*zis kan zot andeor ki zot konn Moris so valer*)!'

'The lagoon around our island is shallow and swarming with fish,' he told him. 'All we need to do is wade in the water and help ourselves. But there's one golden rule: we must never wade barefoot in the lagoon or on the reef. The most dangerous creature in these shallow lagoons is the stonefish (*laf labou*). He is dark and gray and it's very difficult to see him in the water against the sand and the coral. He's got spikes on his back which are very poisonous. Treading on him is very painful and can be fatal. Therefore the least you can do is make matting soles and tie them to your feet.'

Xara and Manuel loved wading in the lagoon and catching fish. Only trouble was there were too many of them fighting over the bait. Bonefish and trevally (*karang*) were among the most voracious. These fish weighed anything between 15 to 40 kg.

8

Xara and Manuel used to catch and release them and kept only one or two *kapitenn* and *damberi*. They often had to frighten away first-grade fish to catch the super-grade fish they fancied for their dinner.

Manuel was reminded of how a fisherman had boasted about the fish-abounding lagoons of St Brandon:

'Here In Mauritius, you must push away water to get fish (*bizin pous dilo pou gagn poson*). In Saint Brandon, you must push away fish to get water *(bizin pous poson pou gagn dilo*)!'

Manuel had thought the man was exaggerating. But he wasn't.

As a matter of fact, in some places in their island, the water was so solid with shrimp that there was hardly any room for water!

Xara enjoyed sharing with Manuel the things that he liked doing. One day, at low tide, at the hour of sunset, they waded to the shallow table of the main reef and stood on its very edge where the water drops precipitously to unknown depths. They stood there looking into the deep ocean, watching the sea darken to cobalt blue in the twilight. As darkness fell, thousands of rock lobsters were swept over the reef by the incoming tide, and scuttled around their ankles, over coral and crannies, antennae twitching and flicking.

All they had to do was fill their sacks. But they didn't bother. Rock lobsters were not their cup of tea. The reef crawled with large blue and green striped lobsters, crab and shellfish and they had the pick of the very best crustaceans under the sun.

During one of their outings, they made an interesting discovery. They had thought that Manuel's pirogue had been smashed up and dismembered by the coral rocks and swept back into the open sea by the outgoing tide. But that was not the case. The boy's pirogue had been swept by the waves and tossed high on the beach, half-buried in the sand.

9

Manuel was crestfallen to find that the pirogue had been badly battered and its sides ripped open.

'Sorry Manuel,' Xara sympathised, 'the boat is as good as useless.'

'Please *tonton* (uncle),' Manuel pleaded, 'we aren't going to live on this island forever. There must be something we can do to go back home.'

'Sorry Manuel, we don't have the tools nor the materials to repair the boat and make it seaworthy. There's no tree on this island we can use for timber except coco palms and filaos. For a boat we need hard timber. In any case, we can't face the sea in a pirogue.'

'But we can repair the boat and explore the lagoon,' Manuel pleaded. There are other islands in the lagoon. People could be living on one of them. If we try surely God will help us.'

But Xara remained deaf to Manuel's pleas. Every time Manuel brought up the subject, Xara grunted some excuse and changed the subject. When Manuel insisted, Xara glared at him threateningly.

One day, early in the morning when the sea was calm and the water clear as crystal, they were wading over the reef when Manuel saw a big blue and green lobster in a crevice.

'Our favourite food,' he shouted. 'I'll go get it for lunch.'

'Watch your feet. The coral's quite sharp.'

Manuel waded up to the lobster and was almost there when he screamed and fell back thrashing helplessly. Xara quickly turned him on his back and hauled him to the shore. He laid him on the sand and examined the soles of his feet.

The purplish punctures on the soles of one of Manuel's feet confirmed Xara's worst fears.

'Stonefish!' he cursed.

Manuel's foot had begun to swell. Xara poured the strong liquor he made from fermented coconut water down Manuel's throat. Then he enlarged the punctures with his knife and began to suck the poison out. Manuel was writhing and twitching in great pain. There was no antidote on the island to fight the poison, nor any painkiller to soothe the pain. Manuel was delirious and burning with fever.

'Ma, where are you? Why have you left me? Don't leave me alone!' Manuel called several times. 'Pa, come back, don't go. I'm scared!

'Where's Patrice? Where's Suzy? Don't leave me alone. I want to go home. I want to go home!'

There was nothing more Xara could do except press wet green leaves on Manuel's forehead to bring down his temperature.

Then, Xara did something he had not done for years. He closed his eyes and began to pray.

YASMINE

Xara sat by Manuel's side and gazed at the delirious child with infinite sadness. He found himself thinking of his wife, Yasmine. Ever since he had been on the island he had tried not to think of her. But watching Manuel hanging between life and death for the last three days, he found himself recalling the first time he had met his wife and fallen hopelessly in love with her.

Xara came from a fisherman's family and lived in the thatched cottage behind Yasmine's father's beach bungalow. He used to take the family out during the summer holidays to the coral pools among the reef to swim and to snorkel. He had grown up loving her secretly and knew that his love was hopeless until

11

one day, while they were alone in the boat, Yasmine had caught him looking at her.

'Why do you always look at me when you think I'm not looking?' Yasmine asked him.

'Do I?'

'Yes you do. And when I catch you looking at me, you look away as if you did something wrong.'

'How do you know I look at you if you're not looking?'

'I don't have to see you looking at me. I feel your eyes all over me. You don't have to feel guilty. I also look at you when you're not looking. I've known you since we were children. My parents came regularly to spend the summer holidays here in this bungalow. I had no one of my age to play with except you. I loved coming here because of the sea, and also because of you. Then as we grew up, I didn't see you that often. I thought you were avoiding me. And then one day, my parents decided to take their friends on an outing to *l'Ile aux Cerfs* (Stag Island). On our way, my dad asked you to take us to *La Fosse aux Requins* (Sharks' Cauldron).

It was hot on board and on a sudden impulse I bent over the side of the boat and dipped my fingers into the water.

'What are you doing!' my mum screamed. 'This place must be crawling with sharks!'

I quickly pulled my hand out of the water.

'Look over there!' my father pointed excitedly, *La Fosse aux Requins*!'

'Why is this place called *La Fosse aux Requins* !' someone asked.

'The French *colons* (colonists) gave it this name because in this place, there's a deep crater in the sea-bed, and in colonial times, the dead bodies of slaves were secretly dumped here

12

and devoured by sharks that had adopted it as one of their favourite feeding grounds.'

'I peered fearfully into the water, but instead of sharks I saw a beautiful double harp shell wedged on a coral ledge on the rim of the crater, some forty feet under the boat.

'A double harp!' I exclaimed, 'just the shell I've been dying for to complete my collection of tropical shells!'

Without saying a word you dived into the water. We could see you heading straight for the shell.

From out of the blue depths some large grey shapes began to materialise.

"He's mad!" my father shouted, horrified.

All those on board held their breath.

My heart was pounding.

"Come back! Come back!" I shouted, terrified and holding tightly to my mum's arm, my nails clawing into her flesh.

'From the corner of my eyes, I could make out about a dozen grey shapes streaking across the steep crater and circling around you.

But before they could attack, you had picked up the shell and had shot up like an arrow and leapt on board. We could hear the heavy thuds as the sharks lunged under the boat and along its sides, enraged at being deprived of their lunch.

'You held the shell like an Olympic champion holds his trophy and offered it to me. It is the most precious present I've ever received in my life. I have treasured it as a token of our love.'

Yasmine told Xara that since that day she could no longer hide her love for him from herself.

Xara and Yasmine were both happy but also terrified of their love for each other.

Since they knew her parents would never accept him in the family, one day they ran away, got married secretly and lived in a small rented house in the village of Grand Port. Xara's best friend, Fazlai, lived there and he was the only one, apart from his mother, that he had trusted with his secret.

Oh God! he had loved her so much, she was his reason for living. She looked so sweet and so fragile. He had vowed he would protect her all his life and allow nothing to harm her. He dreamt of giving her a house of their own where they would bring up their children. This is why he contracted to work on the fishing boats and stayed away for months at a time. He hoped to make as much money as he could while he was still young and in good health.

Yasmine had often told him she was scared of the dark and could not bear to be left alone at night. And what was worse, she was terrified of thunder. As a child she had always covered her ears and run to her mother and clung to her in terror during thunderstorms. But Xara had laughed away her fears.

'Yasmine,' he chided her, 'you're no longer a child. There's nothing to fear. My mother doesn't live far from here. She has promised to come and live with you when I'm away. And if there's a problem, you can always send for Fazlai. He's my best friend. We can always count on him.

'I cannot make much money here. The sea is my world and I've practically lived in boats all my life. They offer me good wages on the fishing boats. I don't like to be away from you. What is more, life on the fishing boats is hard and dangerous. The sea is always unpredictable and the conditions on the boats and in the fishing stations on those remote islands are not very pleasant. To make matters worse, they are not very choosy about the people they recruit. Some of them can be violent and dangerous. A few of them are criminals hiding from the police. You see this fishing knife. I always carry it with me if I have to defend myself. But you must not fear. I can look after myself. I hate being away from you just as much as you. I'm telling you all this so you can see I'm doing my very best to be worthy of you. I'm sure you too can put up with all these hardships for some time. If you really love me, you will be able to overcome all your fears. I promise you as soon as I make enough money I'm going to build our house and spend all my time with you.'

He remembered that night when he had come back sooner than expected. His ship had an engine problem and was not expected to leave before two days. He had hastened home overjoyed to be able to spend two more days with his wife, specially as she had told him that morning that she was with child. How they had argued over the baby's name!
We'll call him Zayn.
No, it's going to be a girl. We'll call her Shabnam.
He was the happiest man on earth.

He opened the door quietly hoping to surprise her. Yasmine was reclining on the couch and Fazlai was bending over her, his face pressed against her belly. When they saw him, they sprang apart.
'Yasmine was scared of the thunder and called me,' Fazlai stammered. But Xara wasn't listening. Everything happened very quickly. He took out the knife he always carried with him and lunged at him. Fazlai backed away and tried to reason with him.
'I was listening to your baby kicking inside Yasmine's belly. It's not what you think... '

15

He didn't have time to finish. Xara stabbed him several times. Yasmine screamed. He knocked her down and stood over her with the bloodied knife in his hand.

'Don't kill me, please don't. We didn't do anything wrong. Think of our baby. Oh God, please save my baby!'

'You whore, I lived only for you. I kill myself working to make you happy. And the moment my back is turned you jump into bed with my best friend. Go join him in hell ! ' He plunged the knife into her chest.

He could still remember the fierce flashes of lightning and the deafening rolls of thunder that went crashing across the sky as he made his way back to the harbour and embarked on one of the fishing boats bound for the Nazareth banks.

It was the first time since that terrible night, three years ago, that he had thought of her and the baby. He had killed both mother and child. What fault had the unborn baby committed? It was innocent. And he had killed an innocent baby. And what if Fazlai and Yasmine had been telling the truth and hadn't done anything wrong? He had never wanted to think about it before. It was too monstrous a thought to bear. This is why he had hidden away on the island and never wanted to leave.

He thought of his mother. She had placed great hopes in him. What had he brought her? Only pain and suffering. He didn't even know whether she was alive or dead.

'What a mess. Oh God what a bloody mess I've made of my life! If only I could make up a little for all the harm I've done.' He cried bitterly and deep sobs racked his body.

He was brought back to the present with Manuel moaning and calling for his mother.

He looked so young and innocent. He didn't deserve to die at such a tender age. A great wave of tenderness for the child

16

swept over Xara. He realised that he had grown fond of him and cared for him like his own son. He had a chance of making up a little for the terrible harm he had done by helping Manuel. He had been very selfish and had thought only of himself. But he had no right to imprison Manuel and keep him on the island away from the people he loved.

Xara had worked the shoals and sandbanks of Capricorn before and knew that he had been marooned on one of the islands of the Saint Brandon archipelago. He also knew that with a pirogue he could try and reach Raphael Island where there was a fishing station which was regularly visited by schooners from Mauritius. He decided that if Manuel survived he would try and get him to the station from where he could return to Mauritius.

He knew that he was risking arrest and death by hanging if someone recognised him. But it was a risk he was willing to take.

SAILING THE LAGOON

Xara watched over Manuel all the time, not daring to fall asleep, as if death was waiting for the moment when he would not be watching to take Manuel away. He refused to fall asleep and stayed awake for three days and three nights.

On the fourth morning the swelling went down and the fever began to leave Manuel.

'It's a miracle!' Xara thought. 'In most cases the wound inflicted by the stonefish would have been fatal.'

Xara had Manuel swallow a broth of shellfish and bird soup and remained by his side nursing him and feeding him back to health.

When Manuel had recovered completely, Xara took him to where the pirogue lay on its side almost totally covered by sand. 'What about helping me right up the boat?' Xara said.

'Do you mean we're going to repair the boat?' Manuel asked, his eyes dancing with excitement.

'We can always try, but it's not going to be easy. Let's go pick anything we find that we can use for repairing the boat: pieces of wood, nails, canvas and iron from the abandoned buildings. We can make tools from coral and shells.'

Weeks and months passed, and slowly and patiently they worked on the boat.

When they thought it was nearly ready they pushed it in the water and danced with joy when it remained afloat.

They made ropes from dried coconut husks and sails out of dried coconut fronds. They used palm fibre for bindings and lashings.

They cut down two long poles from filao trees to propel the boat in shallow water and two oars from their gnarled roots to paddle the boat in deeper water.

One fine summer morning when the sky was clear, the wind fair and steady, they went down to the beach, pushed out the boat, pushed off from the beach and headed for a grey smudge in the distance,

The water on their left towards the break in the reef was deep and blue, but on their right the water was shallow and crystal-clear. They kept to the shallow water as much as possible skirting coral formations of strange shapes and sizes. Some looked like giant mushrooms and cauliflowers; others like sculpted roses and camellias. There were coral resembling huge plates and quaint plants. In places there were forests of stag horns in and out of which darted myriads of brightly coloured fish.

In some places, attached like blossoms to the coral 'bushes', diaphanous sea anemones swayed with the current. In other places the sandy bottom was strewn with spiky sea urchins, pink starfish, violet-lipped clams and fat sea cucumbers (*banbara*).

'Not unlike our underwater gardens in Mauritius,' Manuel remarked, 'only larger, clearer and more colourful.'

Occasionally, sea turtles glided off in the turquoise waters, swifter than their pirogue.

At times they had to paddle over deep pools where the water was so clear they could see colonies of shells on the seafloor. Some of the bigger pools even had manta rays and sharks swimming in them.

As they progressed, a chain of islets gradually took shape on the horizon. A few were mere humps of sand and coral, most were small, but there was a bigger one at one end of the chain.

Except for some bushes, thickets and palms, there was nothing of interest on the little islets. Xara and Manuel spent the night on one of them and in the morning, after a light meal, they pushed off in their pirogue and made for the bigger one.

RAPHAEL ISLAND

There were definite signs of human activity on the island: three canoes were lying close together on the shore; coconuts, chopped open, lay spread on the ground; a number of long fishing nets were hanging from the trees to dry. But apart from a gaggle of hens running around digging for worms, and two dogs lying flat on the ground in the shade of a palm tree, the place was empty.

'Houses ahead,' announced Xara. 'Let's watch from behind a tree and try to figure out what to do.'

19

Thirty minutes nothing happened. They approached one of the buildings and read from a signboard 'Manager's Office'.

'Manuel, I will do all the talking and you will talk as little as possible and that too only when you are talked to, okay?'

The door was open and they walked in. Monsieur Raoul Leboeuf, the manager, was sitting behind his desk. When he saw Xara, he fixed his gaze on his face as if he was trying to remember something.

'Who are you?' he snorted, 'haven't I seen you before?'

'On TV perhaps,' Xara joked trying to keep the panic out of his voice. 'They call me Zorba and this boy here is Manuel, my nephew.' Xara, of course, didn't want anyone to know his real name.

'What are you doing on my island?'

'We were out fishing off the coast of Grand Gaube and were driven by the wind and the current far from Mauritius. After drifting many days in the open sea, we were swept by a strong current and shipwrecked on an island a few kilometres from here. We lived on the island for many months and after repairing our boat we set out hoping to find an island that is inhabited. And here we are.'

'I heard about this fisherman who went out fishing with his son and they never came back. You're very lucky you survived. Now what do you want from me?'

'Manuel misses his parents and his friends. He wants to go back home. As for me, I'm not in a hurry. I'm an experienced fisherman. I'll be quite happy to work for you and earn some money first and decide later.'

'This is the cyclone season and we have no communication with Mauritius until June,' Leboeuf told them. *'La Perle II* isn't expected here before four to five months and it isn't leaving for

20

Mauritius until we have enough fish. That can be in six months, even longer depending on the weather.'

'I'll be quite happy to work for my passage back,' said Manuel.

'That's okay with me,' the manager said. 'We don't ask many questions here and we can always use two additional pairs of hands. Always remember I'm the boss around here. I make the rules and you do as you're told. Is that clear?'

'Very clear.'

'Wait here, I'm going to arrange for your lodgings and tell you all you need to know later.'

Leboeuf then got up, went outside his office, and they could hear him shouting. A few minutes later he walked back into his office accompanied by one of his men.

'Octave, this man says he is Zorba and this boy here is Manuel, his nephew. They will be with us for some time. I want you to show them round and arrange for them to live with you. But first we have to go to the beach. The fishermen are coming in.'

On the way to the beach, Octave told them that Leboeuf managed the affairs of the St Brandon Fishing Company which exploits the islets of the St Brandon archipelago and the Nazareth bank.

'He pretends he's the big boss and bullies all of us around. The real boss, Philippe Legris, sits in his office in Mauritius and occasionally visits the station. When he's around, Leboeuf is as meek as a lamb. "Yes Sir, no Sir, you're absolutely right Sir. Can I kiss your ass, Sir!" That's Leboeuf for you! I'm a fisherman but because I can read and write he uses me as some kind of an all-purpose servant. When I'm not out fishing I do most of his work. But it doesn't bother me. I get more than he thinks out of this arrangement.

'I help him note down the catch of the day and record the number of kilos of fish and the sum each fisherman has earned.

After weighing, we put the fish in a barrel of seawater. The next day, we transfer the fish onto a long concrete table to dry in the sun. Once dried, the fish is stored in big sacks and shipped to Mauritius later.'

'Here they come!' Octave pointed at the lagoon.

There on the turquoise water a small flotilla of small craft was heading for the beach.

'You wait for me here. I'm going down to help Leboeuf and I'll be with you in a jiffy.'

By late afternoon, after settling them down in his shack, Octave asked them if there was anything special they fancied for dinner.

'Oh yes, please. I've been living on fish for such a long time; sometimes I feel scales growing on my skin! Chicken curry would be fine!' Xara said, licking his lips.

'Oh yes, please, chicken curry would be great!' Manuel pleaded, his mouth watering.

'With green chili if you please!'

'Consider it done.'

At about 6 p.m., Octave climbed up a tree where a veteran cock was roosting. When he reached out to grab it, the cock, sensing death knocking at its door, in a startled flurry of feathers and screeches, flew off the tree and bolted for the beach followed by Octave, Xara and Manuel in hot pursuit. The cock was more than a match for the three of them as it dribbled, feinted and slipped between their legs to take refuge in the thickets. The chase was finally abandoned after it grew too dark to see.

When they returned to the shack, they flopped down on a wooden bench completely exhausted.

'My folk back home will be tickled to death when I tell them I spent my first night in Raphael Island running after a cock!' Manuel laughed.

22

'Sorry,' Octave mumbled in apology. 'Sorry, the blasted cock escaped *(kok-la finn bouré)*! It's fish again for dinner.'

'Fish again *(ankor poson)*'! lamented Manuel.

'How about some local toddy we make out of fermented coconut milk?' Octave proposed. 'But I warn you. Go easy on it. It kicks harder than a mule!'

'Where's the chili you promised us?' Xara asked when dinner was served. 'The chili also has bolted (p*ima ousi finn bouré*)!

'Oh I forgot,' Octave said. He went out and placed a potted chili plant on the table.

'Help yourself to fresh chili straight from the tree!' he said with a flourish.

'As you can see, what's common in Mauritius is a luxury here, and what's common here is a luxury in Mauritius. But still, I can't understand those weathermen in the met station down the street.'

'What about them?' enquired Manuel.

'Well, they come out here on a four-month roster. You'd think they'd help themselves to the best seafood in the world, wouldn't you? But no no no not them. They live only on canned tunas, canned sardines, dried fish and *minn Apollo* (Apollo noodles) they bring with them from Mauritius! Just imagine!'

'What about some salad?' Xara suggested.

'No problem. Just cut down a coconut palm, make salad with its heart. But you have to kill a tree to make a salad. No one here is allowed to kill a coconut tree except, of course, Leboeuf. I kill the tree and make salad for him, and of course, I keep the best part for me, *kifer mo koz manti ha! ha! ha* (I've got nothing to hide, ha! ha! ha)! I'll get some for you.'

After dinner Octave took them to the recreation room where the fishermen assembled to watch a videotaped film.

Manuel was over the moon!

Xara wanted to know more about life on the island. He was a man in hiding and had to decide whether to return to Mauritius and run the risk of getting life, or remain on the island until it was safe for him to return. He was told that the living conditions were not too bad.

'There are about 35 contract workers living on the island, mostly Mauritian but also from Rodrigues and Seychelles,' Octave told him. 'Most of the fishermen come here for the money. They stay here for three months or more and go home for short breaks.'
'Here, life is tough. You get up everyday at 4.30 a.m. Some days, when the weather is bad, you don't catch anything. Many fishermen feel like prisoners living in exile. They miss their wives and their children.
I've been here several times for periods of six months to one year. Every time I come, I leave my heart behind in Mauritius. This time I miss my family even more than before. I long to go back home to Baie du Tombeau. My wife is sick and I want to be by her side. I've promised her this is going to be my last contract. I'm never going to leave her again.'
'Are women allowed to accompany their husbands here?' Xara asked.
'They tried it once. But it didn't work,' Octave said. 'Many years ago, wives were allowed to join their husbands. But there was big trouble. The husbands refused to go fishing and leave their wives behind with non-fishing staff. Eventually several fishermen died in knife fights and even some of the women got killed.'
Manuel got a job drying, salting and packing fish in sacks to be shipped to Mauritius. Xara went out with Octave and another

fisherman, Isidore, in a pirogue to fish with handlines. He rarely came back with less than 100 kg of fish thus earning about Rs 900, or Rs 9 per kg.

Fishing the sandbanks was not easy and could also be dangerous, especially during the cyclone season. One day, Xara and his two companions were fishing the Nazareth bank and had caught a record number of *kapitenn* and *damberi* when the weather suddenly changed for the worse, with winds gusting at over 100 km per hour. The sea was rising and thousands of sea-birds were flying back home o their nests.

'Let's take shelter on the nearest island,' Xara said. 'I will never forget what my old man used to say: "Never remain on the sea when sea-birds are leaving it."

'What about all the fish we have caught?' Isidore asked. 'If we wait out the cyclone on an island, they'll all go bad, and we'll have to throw away the lot of them.'

'That's too bad,' Octave said. 'But 'I don't think we'll be able to make it to Raphael before sunset in this lousy weather. We'd better take shelter on the nearest island.'

'There's something we can do,' Xara said. 'The two of you can shelter on an island. I'll try to reach Raphael on my own and transfer the fish to the cold storage. I shall come and pick you up as soon as the weather clears up.'

Octave and Isidore got off on an island where there was a shelter for stray fishermen. Xara made it to Raphael and waited for the weather to get better. But the weather got worse as a full-scale tropical cyclone hit the archipelago. The sea growled like a fearsome sea monster threatening to swallow the entire archipelago. Then the rain came, torrents of it, swept by cyclonic winds, lashing the islands ruthlessly for two full days and nights.

Then, slowly, the cyclone left St Brandon and moved on to terrorise other islands of the Indian Ocean. The wind dropped, the rain ceased. Everything went back to normal. The sun shone bright and the sea became calm and inviting as ever.

When Xara went back to pick up his companions, the island had simply disappeared. The entire island had been swept away by the cyclone.

Two more names were added to the long list of fishermen lost at sea.

Five months passed and *La Perle II* had come and after loading up she was sailing back to Mauritius the next day.

That night Xara and Manuel could not sleep. They lay listening to the distant boom on the surf, and the whispering of the wind through the trees.

'*Tonton* (Uncle), God has listened to my prayers,' Manuel said. 'At last, I'm going back home.'

'Yes Manuel, I'm very happy for you.'

' But *tonton*, you can also go back home.'

'Not now. Later perhaps.'

'*Tonton*, how could you live alone for such a long time? Don't you have anybody in Mauritius? Don't you have a wife and children? Don't you have a mother, a father, brothers and sisters? You are not dead. You are still alive. Just imagine how happy they'll be when they see you are still alive!'

'I have no one. You go. I'll work for a bit, make some money. When I have enough money, I'll go back.'

'*Tonton*, promise me you'll come and see me. You know where I live.'

'You'll be the first person I'll come to see, I promise. You are like a son to me.'

'*Tonton*, I will never forget you. You saved my life many times. I have lost my father. God has sent you to me. You are like a father to me. I don't want to lose my father a second time.'

It was time to leave. *La Perle II* was ready to steam away.

Manuel was crying as he climbed on board.

Then the hooter sounded, the gangway was raised, ropes were cast off and *La Perle II* headed for the open sea.

'Come back. I'll be waiting for you. Come back!' Manuel called out as the ship started on her twenty four hour voyage to Mauritius.

Manuel stood on the deck waving goodbye until the island faded away in the distance.

When *La Perle II* was out of sight, Xara was returning to his quarters when from the corner of his eyes he saw Leboeuf in animated conversation with two officials of the St Brandon Fishing Company who had stayed behind on the island. He could see them looking in his direction and following him with their eyes. He knew that Leboeuf had been asking questions about him and suspected him to be a fugitive from justice. He could not run the risk of being arrested and sent back to Mauritius to face trial.

Rather than rot in prison for the rest of his life, Xara preferred to brave the dangers of the open sea and die if necessary; or if he survived, to live the rest of his life on one of those solitary islands of the Indian Ocean.

***

FISHY STORIES

Every Sunday morning at the crack of dawn, I picked up Sam Pyndiah who had initiated me into the wonders of our underwater world, and drove to the small fishing village of Black River on the west coast of the island, where we would borrow Ton Maxim's pirogue and sail out through the pass of *Larmoni*, about one kilometre from shore, anchor some 30 yards from the outer reef, fish to our heart's content, and come back home with a variety of our preferred seafood - super-grade fish, octopus, calamari and lobster - with which we would regale family and friends.

After some time many friends wanted to join our fishing outings. We therefore got ten of the keenest wannabe *spearos*, pooled our savings to buy a pirogue which we could use for all types of aquatic activities - sailing, snorkelling, spear-fishing, fishing with line and fish-trap, and also, weather-permitting, big game fishing.
A pirogue had many advantages. It was the cheapest craft available, simple to handle on which we could fish on either ends, and along both sides of its length. But Ton Maxim advised against it.

'You don't want a pirogue to earn a living like we fishermen do,' he said.
'You want a boat for sport and pleasure. You want a boat in which you can take your friends and also your girlfriends out not only for fishing, but also for swimming, snorkelling, diving, and also for all sorts of outings.

'Remember when you're out on the sea and the sun is grilling you, there's no tree there in whose shade you can hide *(kan to dan lamer an plin soley, pena pié pou donn twa lonbraz)*! You don't want your girlfriend to go out fair and come back zulu *(to palé to kopinn alé kler, retourné zulu)!*

'And don't forget to bring a large hat with you,' he cautioned.

Taking into consideration our limited resources, Ton maxim advised us to buy *enn bato demi-ponté* (a small boat with a small cabin) which would be ideal for fishing and snorkelling in the lagoon and also outside the reef, in whose small cabin we could rest when we felt like it, sheltered from the sun.

And this is what we did. We acquired a cute little boat and called her *La Sirène*, because she never ceased to enchant and beguile us. The call of the sea was irresistible and she was the one that took us to her bosom.

Our infatuation with the sea was such that we often threw caution to the winds and even put our lives at risk. I'm not proud to say that once we had planned to go out, and had already reached our base on the coast, and got everything ready, nothing could have made us change our minds. Weather conditions might change for the worst, rain might start to pour out of the heavens, we just had to be out there amidst the winds and waves. Only after we had tasted the fury of the elements and felt death breathing down our necks that we sobered down and hightailed it to the safety of the shore, immensely relieved to feel the solid earth beneath our feet, swearing never again to go back in again in bad weather. But we always did. We must consider ourselves very lucky we survived to tell the tale.

Once, we were preparing to go out when the met station issued a cyclone warning class 2, in anticipation of a class 3 cyclone warning to be issued later in the afternoon. All boats were supposed to be out of the water and secured by ropes on the shore. The sea was calm, and a few water-skiers and windsurfers were still indulging their favourite sport.

'These weathermen are jackasses *(zot bann farser)*!' we joked as we pushed out to sea and stationed *La Sirène* about 40 yards from the reef. Within minutes the weather turned nasty. Seven-foot waves rolled in from the open sea and started battering *La Sirène*, driving her relentlessly against the reef. We all clung desperately to her sides and, forgetting our own safety, we dived around and underneath her in an attempt to protect her from the coral outcrops and steer her through the canals that crisscrossed the reef until we were delivered into the calmer waters of the lagoon.

Our group of ten came to be known as the Black River Gang and initially included one member who later became a Minister of Fisheries; three others who later became a prominent businessman, an entrepreneur and an industrialist respectiely; two were teachers, two male nurses; and two unemployed young men *(dé somer)*. At the time we were all ordinary citizens struggling to live off our modest wages. The group later expanded into a large fraternity that included Europeans, Americans, Canadians, and members of many other nationalities both male and female.

Our group had snorkelled and fished most of the reefs around the island, especially those stretching off Le Morne, La Mivoie and Albion in the west coast; and those off Trou aux Biches, Mon Choisy, Grand Baie and Cap Malheureux in the north. We had reconnoitred some of the reefs in the east - off Poste

30

Lafayette, Belmar and Palmar, but had found them too sombre and spooky for our taste. We had kept away from the reefs of the south and south west, because of the high winds, powerful rollers and treacherous currents.

We normally pushed off to sea around 6 a.m., snorkelled and fished until about noon, came back to shore, grilled and ate some of the fish we had caught, rested for an hour or so, and pushed off to sea again.

We would come back when the sun was about to sink into the sea, or as Ton Maxim liked to say with a smile *'kan lamer pé aval soley* (when the sea is swallowing the sun).' At that hour, the sun would be lying low on the horizon, painting the whole western sky red, orange, crimson, indigo and violet. That was also the hour when we entered the pass accompanied by a school of friendly dolphins and a flight of seagulls - the dolphins racing us well inside the pass, leaping, romping and gambolling around our boat; the seagulls shrieking, circling and hovering all around us.

When the dolphins had said their goodbyes and had gone to their sleeping quarters off Tamarin Bay, and the seagulls had winged their way to their mountain dormitories, we rapped on the bulwarks with short wooden clubs. The raucus startled mullet and flying fish that leapt and flew in their hundreds across our bows, falling and flapping in their dozens into our boat, providing us with plenty of fresh fish that we shared out among the fishermen's children, among whom Ti Rouget, Alex and Ti Jean, who grew up to be good fishermen and skippers in their own right.

I wish to make it clear here that there was much more to our expeditions than fish. There was the exhilaration of the open sea, the magical underwater world, the thrills of discovery, the excitement of the hunt, the warm comradeship and the 'fantastic' stories which grew more and more fantastic every time we told and retold them to family and friends around a campfire and on other social occasions.

One member of the group was Prem Chopra, PC for short, that I had known from my childhood days in Port Louis. PC had a chip on his shoulder. He always wanted to impress upon others that he was better than what he actually was. Since he cut a poor figure in the classroom, he was always trying, by fair or foul means, to compensate for his failure at school by his 'superiority' outside the school

When we started spear-fishing, PC made it a point to be one up on all of us. He was, for example, the only one to wear a full-length wetsuit with large flexible diving fins, weight belt and a large professional diver's knife strapped to his leg. He had an expensive rubber-powered spear-gun and a stainless steel spear which gave him an edge over the rest of us. Fortunately there was more to spear-fishing than equipment and fancy suits. And that was skill, experience and nerve.

When he joined our group PC almost succeeded in turning our outings into contests of skill and derring-do. And for some reason beyond my comprehension, he picked me as his favourite rival. I am normally an easygoing guy always ready to help others but PC's constant big-headedness began to get on my nerves and I enjoyed pricking his inflated ego whenever I had a chance. That was not a difficult thing to do as even the sea seemed to conspire in cutting him down to size.

Once, for example, we had gone out line-fishing at night in a pirogue. We had agreed the following bets between us:
The one who catches the first fish wins Rs 200;
The one who catches the biggest fish wins Rs 200;
The one who catches more fish wins Rs200;
The one who catches the best quality fish wins Rs200.
Duration of the competition: 6.30 p.m. to midnight.

We anchored about 100 metres off *Pwint Gro Piké* facing Le Morne. After fishing for five solid hours I caught one small *viel* weighing less than half a pound. PC had managed to catch nothing!
On the strength of that wretched little fish, I won on all counts and was entitled to collect Rs 800 from PC!
I'm still waiting!
You could argue that I was entitled to only Rs 200 as only the first condition applied in this case. The other conditions could only apply if both of us had caught at least one fish each to allow for comparisons!

Another time, I shot and caught a ten-pound *kapitenn blé*. It was the best catch we had made and PC tried very hard to beat my record.
One day, in my absence, PC speared a 35-pound stingray which would be rated a better catch than mine.
PC was as happy as a pig in shit. His happiness was marred by the fact that I wasn't there when it happened.
'The bastard knew I was going to catch a big fish today. That's why he didn't turn up!' he told everyone who would listen to him.

33

He had its length, breadth and weight measured and recorded. He got Ton Maxim and his sons, Robert and Regis, to stand as witnesses. He had photos taken of himself posing with his trophy.

When we met the following week, I pretended to doubt his story. 'I knew you would say I'm making it up, that it never happened. But I can prove to you it really did happen,' he said. When I was confronted with the photos and the testimony of Ton Maxim, Robert and Regis, I said,
'Maybe it's true. Maybe it's not true. But I wasn't there when it happened, so it doesn't count.'

My refusal to recognise his catch stuck in PC's throat like a fish bone, and every time we went out spear-fishing PC did not hesitate to go after bigger fish in deeper water at depths which were beyond his limits.

But while we went out spear-fishing for sport and pleasure, there were unscrupulous individuals who used spear-fishing as a front to dynamite the habitat of the fish and wreak irreparable damage to fish and marine life. We could see them leaving in boats in the morning ostensibly to spear-fish but in reality to dynamite many areas of the reef. We could also see them coming back to shore, their pirogues loaded to the brim with sacks upon sacks of fish and crustaceans that they had killed in their hundreds, only about one third of which they could collect, while hundreds more sank to the bottom of the sea or were carried away by the current to the open sea.

The indiscriminate destruction of the fish and their habitat could no longer be tolerated and when sometime in the late seventies,

34

Government passed a law banning spear- fishing in Mauritian waters, we supported the ban although it struck at the very core of our romance with the sea. We had got used to snorkelling and diving in all sorts of places with a gun in our hand. But without a gun, we felt puny, unsafe and vulnerable.

SHOOT TO SAVE

On the eve of the day when the law was to come into effect, we decided to hold a spear- fishing competition, the winner to be proclaimed the *champion des champions (the champ)*.

The rules were carefully explained to all the participants, ten in all.
Points were allocated for the number of fish caught, their size and quality:
3 points per pound for first-grade fish - *viel rouz, mama rouz, milatres, sakrechien, vakoa, gelpavé, kapitenn, damberi etc.*
2 points per pound for second-grade fish - *rouzé, karang, katover, kato rouz, kordonié, makro, madras, karandinn etc.*
I point per pound for sub-standard fish - *lion boutey, lantern, madam tonbé, karp, savonet etc.*
A lobster counted 4 points per pound, calamari 3 points and octopus 2 points.
Pelagic fish like tuna, wahoo *(bekinn)*, dorado, barracuda *(tazar)*, ray, sailfish, marlin and the like counted 3 points per pound.
Bonus of 10 points for fish weighing over 10 lbs.
Bonus of 15 points for fish over 20 lbs.
Bonus of 20 points for fish over 30 lbs.
Penalty for shooting fish under 1 lb: -3 points.

Penalty for shooting octopus, calamari and crayfish under 1 lb: -
10 points.
Starting time: 6.30 a.m.
Closing time: 1 p.m.

Ton Maxim and his two sons, Robert and Regis, acted as Jury.
Sam Pyndiah acted as Advisor to the Jury. The decision of the
Jury was final.

Over the years everyone had developed his own style and
technique of fishing:
Some liked to swim along the reef among the coral formations,
and go mainly for coral fish that swam in and out of the coral
gardens or that swayed and floated in the current.
Others liked to explore fissures and cavities, or dived to the
bottom of the coral structures, reach out into grottoes and
caves.
There were those who chased the fish and shot them as soon
as they were within shooting range.
And there were those who wanted to catch bigger fish and
fished in deeper water.
We pushed off from the beach at 6 a.m. in two pirogues, one
skippered by Regis, the other by Robert. The sea was flat as a
lake and the water clear as crystal. By 6.30, the boats had cast
anchor about 200 metres apart, about 30 yards outside the reef.

I decided I would swim parallel to the reef until I came upon one
of those large crater-like *basins* (pools) that I knew were located
in the area, often as large as a basketball pitch, whose sides
sloped down steeply to a depth of about 100 ft, and fish on its
slopes at a depth of about 25 ft.

These pools were always packed with fish: large green parrotfish, big fat *karang* (trevally), tuna, wahoo, barracuda and enormous rays. The water was transparent blue and you could see far out into the distance and right down to the seabed some 100 ft below.

They were occasionally visited by mean and hungry-looking sharks hunting for food.

The last time I had been there, I didn't dare venture out into the pool. I had hung around the rim and watched hypnotised by the abundance and variety of fish life. Gradually I mustered enough courage and started to swim across the pool.

Suddenly, all the fish that had been quietly swaying with the current or just passing by shot wildly in all directions as a tremor passed through the water. Just then a dark sinister shape, built like a large torpedo, materialised in the blue distance. I didn't wait to take a second look and made it to the safety of my vantage point on the rim of the pool just when the shark, a man-eating tiger shark, passed within 9 feet of my hiding place, in hot pursuit of a 45-pound dorado. I watched rooted to the spot with fear as the shark pounced on his prey and with one swipe of his deadly jaws bit off the body of the fish clean from its head! I normally fished in 20 ft of water and never went below 30 feet. On one occasion, I had shot a ten-pounder and dived to grab him. When I reached below 35 feet, the pressure on my ears was such that my eardrums could have easily burst. And like every diver, I knew that diving at a depth of over 40 feet could even prove fatal.

Since this was a competition I planned to win, I decided I would go after bigger fish in deeper water up to a maximum of 40 feet. I planned to remain at a depth of 20 ft. The nylon string linking my spear to my gun was 25 feet long. Once I had speared a fish, all I had to do was pull him up and string him on my float-line which was tied to a buoy-marker floating on the surface of the water.

When I reached the pool, PC had already stationed himself on its upper slope, and to all intents and purposes, was planning to use the same technique I had banked on using.
I decided to concentrate on fishing and forget about everything else.
I lay motionless on the edge of the immense pool waiting for a sizeable fish to come within reach. There were many large fish sporting in the pool, and as none was coming my way, I decided to swim some distance across, catch two or three good-sized fish to swing the competition in my favour, go back to my vantage point, and lie in wait on the rim of the pool.

When I was 25 ft across the pool, I saw a ten-pound blue parrotfish approach and I began to stalk him. When I was about 20 ft above him I took careful aim and was about to pull the trigger when suddenly the parrotfish disappeared from view and the water under me began to shake and wobble in a most terrifying way. Then I saw something huge flutter right under my nose, about five ft under me. I kicked up to the surface and looked down. I almost jumped out of my skin when I realised that that 'something' was the wing of a giant manta ray that was gliding majestically past ! I had hardly recovered from my shock when I saw a second manta ray, almost as large as the first, glide past just as majestically. In all probability I reasoned, it must have been a male ray and his female companion going quietly about their business.

38

They must have measured over 12 feet long by 7 feet wide, and weighed between 500 and 700 pounds!

After this mind-blowing experience, I decided to lie in wait at my vantage point on the edge of the pool, and go only after fish that came within shooting range.

After some time I saw a large *karang* (trevally) of about 70 lbs approach within reach. I was sorely tempted to shoot him but I knew that a fish that size was way too powerful for me to handle on my own. I remembered the story of how Lai Cheong, one the most experienced spear-fishermen on the island, had speared a 40 pound *karang* and how the latter had dragged him to his death among the coral in deeper water. Lai Cheong, like any other experienced spear-fisher, could have handled a forty pounder, had he not got entangled in his line and cable among the coral as the *karang* thrashed and flailed wildly to escape. I had also been told how Lai Cheong's friends had later retrieved his dead body along with that of the *karang* and had laid them side by side at his wake that night.

With a heavy heart I let the *karang* go and watched him as he cruised around in the pool and swam close to the spot where PC was lying in wait.

I then watched in alarm as PC took aim and pulled the trigger. His spear went through the *karang's* thick skin and bit deep into his flesh. The fish bolted to the depths dragging PC with him in deeper water. PC held on fast and wouldn't let go of his gun. After some time, I could see the gun slip from PC's hands and watched horrified as his body drifted down, limp, unconscious and probably lifeless, weighed down by his weighted belt

I realised it would be reckless of me to try and rescue PC at that depth. After all, we were not the best of friends. As a matter of fact, PC was loudmouthed, bossy, superficial and downright detestable. Even if I tried to save him, chances were I would probably die in the attempt. And yet, I could not sit there and do nothing and live to carry a burden of guilt for the rest of my life.

At that moment, I remembered an amazing true life story I had read of how a champion spear-fisherman had shot his diving companion in the fins, then pulled him up from a depth of about 60 feet and saved him from drowning. But what if I shot PC and killed him? I would most probably be charged with manslaughter and spend the rest of my life in jail.

All this went through my head in a flash. I realised I had to act now before it was too late. Every second could cost PC his life. I stopped thinking and blanking out all considerations for my own safety, I dived down to a depth which I knew was beyond my limits. My lungs were bursting for air and the pressure on my ears and my head was unbearable. I tried to focus and aimed at PC's fins. But my vision was getting blurred and I couldn't get a clear shot at them. I therefore aimed at the fleshy part of PC's thigh and pulled the trigger. The shaft penetrated his thigh and held fast to it as I pulled him up, grabbed his limp and inanimate body, and kicked up to the surface. As I broke through the water, I lifted my gun and screamed for help.

PC was given emergency treatment on Regis's pirogue that had picked us up and rushed to hospital. Incredible but true, he hadn't sustained any serious respiratory or cerebral damage. His lungs and brain were intact, and except for his thigh that had necessitated 16 stitches, he was back on his feet and out of the hospital after 4 days.

Once in a while, when I look back on my life, there are a few things I'm not proud of and I begin to have doubts about myself

40

and the choices I had made. But when I think of that moment when I had acted instinctively to save PC in spite of all the odds to the contrary, something lights up in me and my spirits lift up. That is the moment I prize most in my life and the recollection of that moment gives me the strength to keep fighting for what I believe is right.

In case you're thinking that this experience changed PC, you're wrong. He remained just as loud, as ostentatious, as bossy and as detestable as before and lived to achieve all that he had boasted to achieve - a big house, a seaside bungalow, a fishing launch, a luxury car, a beautiful wife, the summum of earthly joys in short. And all that on a monthly salary about the same as the rest of us! How he managed to do what he did is nobody's business.
Que voulez-vous, c'est la vie!

In case you're wondering who won the spear-fishing competition, here again life played one of the tricks she's fond of playing.
PC and I had technically defaulted.
The prize did not go to the most daring or experienced of the *spearos*. It went to Dave, a pure vegetarian, who was the least daring among us. Dave fished in water not deeper than 15 ft. He didn't go after the fish. He waited for the fish to come to him. He normally hid behind a coral outcrop overhanging a canal on the reef, and had his pick of the fish that came in with the current past his hiding place.

Contrary to what is often said, success seldom goes to the best among us. It very often goes to the least deserving.
Que voulez-vous, c'est la vie!

OCTOPUS BITES

If you think the ban on spear-fishing put an end to our weekly outings you are mistaken. We continued to swim, snorkel and dive along the reef, in the underwater gardens and natural pools studding the reef.

Even after the ban on spear-fishing came into effect, the rivalry between PC and me continued unabated.

We continued to fish, not with a spear gun but with a bamboo pole and line! Mind you, we didn't fish from the boat as traditional fishermen do. We innovated! Whoever said necessity is the mother of invention knew what they were talking about. Donning mask, tube, fins, and armed with a bamboo pole and baited line, a float-line to store the fish we caught and on which was strung a pouch containing our bait, we swam out over the inner and outer reef looking for fish. When we saw fish darting in and out from under a coral plate or from crannies, we would float over them, stretch out our bamboo pole and dangle the baited hook right in front of their noses, and with a swift jerk of our wrist, pull up the fish that had taken our bait.

Sounds easy, doesn't it? But it takes a lot of skill and experience to perfect this particular technique. First you need to know the terrain, so that you fish in an area where coral fish abound. Then you need to be familiar with the ways of the fish. Different species of fish have different habits and lifestyles. For example *viel* (grouper) species always stick close to their coral homes. These fish are always hungry and cannot resist the juicy snacks that float and dangle right before their maws. The problem is there are different kinds of *viel - viel gri, viel rouz, viel kwizinié, viel lisien, viel labou, milatres, mama rouz, krwasan* - weighing anything from half a lb to 25 lbs. Some *viels* are real delicacies, others are not, and a few are even poisonous! You need to know which is which. When they fight over your bait, you need to know how to dissuade the ones you don't want and how to manipulate your line so that the bait lands into the maw of the *viel* you want to hook. There are of course other fish that you can catch with this technique.

It often happens that while we're fishing amidst the coral close to the reef, we see a lobster in its cranny or an octopus in its coral fortress, in which case we go back to the boat and pick up the long harpoon *(gaf)* with which we pierce the creature and prise it out of its home, and throw it into the boat before pushing off again. One could harpoon large edible eels as well except that eels are difficult customers. They writhe and wrap themselves around the harpoon and can inflict serious injuries in their attempt to escape.

One day, PC and I were fishing on the outer reef of Le Morne about 20 metres opposite *Pwint Gro Piké*. We often fished together for security reasons. It is definitely not advisable to fish solo outside the reef. Any number of things could go wrong and you need someone to watch your back. After about an hour or so, I saw PC returning to the boat and coming back with the harpoon that we always keep on board. When he arrived about 10 metres from the reef in relatively shallow water, he stood up on a coral shelf and drove the harpoon with great force into the cranny which an octopus had made his home. He then started twisting and pulling the harpoon. I could see huge tentacles snaking up his harpoon, up his arms, around his chest and neck. I could then see the head of a giant octopus emerging from the water, two cord-like tentacles still clinging to the coral rock while all the other tentacles had fastened on PC's body.

43

The latter was precariously poised on a coral boulder and was being slowly dragged into the water. Before his head disappeared underwater, PC screamed for me to come to his help.

Within seconds I was beside him. I had to attack the creature and cut off the tentacles that had wrapped themselves around PC. I realised that wasn't going to help. The octopus held PC in a vice-like embrace and he wasn't going to let go as long as he was still alive. The only thing to do was to attack and kill the octopus. I pulled my long diving knife that was strapped to my thigh and stabbed him between his two bulbous eyes. The blade of the knife bit hard and deep. The water around churned and blackened as the octopus released his ink sacs in an instinctive bid to confuse and frighten me away. I kept stabbing him through the dark purplish cloud until he was dead.
I then cut off the tentacles that were still wrapped around PC and together we hauled the octopus to the boat.

If you thought PC was grateful I saved his life you'd be quite wrong. Far from it, he was proud of the purplish black blotches across his body and neck and he was looking forward to flaunting them as proofs of his mettle. He insisted that it was he who had harpooned the octopus and that he had beaten the record I had established with the 10-pound *kapitenn blé* I had once speared.
I argued that I had killed the octopus and that it should count as my catch, not his.
Finally we agreed we were both of us *ex aequo* winners of the entire fishing competition which included, among other things, my 10-pound *kapitenn blé*, PC's 35-pound stingray, and the giant octopus we had both caught ! As a bonus, PC agreed to

44

celebrate our victory with our fishermen friends and stand all of us drinks and *gajaks* (snacks) that evening in Wong Chi Man's bar *(bivet)* in Black River Bay.

When PC reached home late that night, he found the main door locked. He didn't stop ringing the bell until his wife, Shirley, opened the door and greeted him with a volley of abuse.

'D'you know what time it is?' she rasped. 'It's 11.30 p.m. I waited for you the whole evening and you didn't even bother to call. What happened?'

PC told her he had a very trying day but it was well worth it. He told her I had at long last conceded defeat, thus putting an end to our long-standing rivalry. He could now sleep in peace at night and she wouldn't have to worry about him coming late from now on.

'Come *mon chouchou, ma chérie*, let's celebrate!' he declared and drew her into his arms.

'To santi pi (you smell awful) !' Shirley pushed him away.

She insisted that he should take a shower before coming to bed. PC hurried into the bathroom, took off his clothes and sang while he showered.

He then hurried into the bedroom. Shirley was already in bed waiting for him. PC dived into the bed beside her and was about to kiss her when she suddenly sat up and pointed to his neck.

'What's this?' she hissed, 'looks like *suçons* (love bites)! How did you get these *suçons*? And the smell ! That's not rum. I know how rum smells. I know that smell. *To santi pi sex* (You reek of sex)!'

Shirley examined his neck, shoulders and arms. There were purplish blotches all over his body.

'What are these? Where do they come from? What woman were you with?'

Shirley threw herself at him, eyes blazing, nails stabbing.

'You rascal, have you no shame! You have a wife in your house, you keep a mistress outside! Get the f... out of my house. Go back to your whore (*fay vorien, to pa onté! To ena to fam dan to lakaz, to gard fam deor! Sorti la mo dir twa. Al res kot to pitin*)!'

'No you don't understand. It's not what it looks like!'

'You rascal, have you no shame! Get out before I murder you!'

'You don't understand. I swear I spent the whole day fishing. I harpooned a big octopus. The octopus did that to me!'

'The octopus gave you love bites! The octopus kissed you on your neck, on your thighs, all over your body! You want me to believe that? Get the f... out of my house!'

Shirley started hitting him and pushing him out of the bedroom.

'You swine,' she hissed, 'you're not going to sleep in this house to-night. Go back to your whore!'

She then grabbed a broom and chased him out of the house.

'*Al dormi ar to fam-ourit* (Go f... your octopus woman)!' she shrieked.

PC kept pleading with her to let him in. But she double-locked the door and didn't want to listen.

PC spent the night *dan kazot poul* (lit. in the poultry shed)!

Epilogue

PC and I later started big-game fishing in earnest. Our catches included bonito, tuna, dorado, *wahoo*, *barracuda*, sailfish and marlin weighing anything between 300 to 750 lbs!

Fishing had established a bond between us and we became good friends.

But you'd be again wrong if you thought we had stopped competing against each other. We didn't compete openly but we kept a secret record of the size and weight of every fish we caught. We also kept photos of our best catches. You never know when you could be challenged and would have to back your claims with hard evidence!

***

MONARCH OF THE FOREST

A Hunting Adventure

'All the sounds of this valley run together into one great echo, a song that is sung by all the spirits of this valley. Only a hunter hears it.'

I have loved the forest for as long as I can remember. This is hardly surprising as I was born and grew up in a thatch-roofed wooden house on the edge of the largest forest in the south-west of the island, stretching for as far as the eyes can see all the way from the thickly canopied mountains down the forested slopes to the low-lying distant sea.

My twin sister also loved the forest but not in the same way as me. As children we spent countless hours wandering down unknown forest trails and wading across hidden streams. But while she felt completely happy taking in the sights, sounds and scents, I couldn't see fruits on a tree without gorging myself on their pulp, and getting drunk on their juices; nor could I see forest animals and fowl without devising ways and means to ensnare or kill them.

While my sister peopled the forest with fauns and fairies, elves and gnomes, and all kinds of magical creatures, I looked for pheasants and partridges, hares and wild boar, and most of all, great antlered stags.

While she bathed in cool springs and rested on river rocks filling her ears with the many voices of their waters, I ransacked rivulets in search of red river shrimp, blue black prawn and big fat *goramié*.

Yes it's true, most of the foods I enjoy eating grow in the forest. Of all meats, I love venison and wild boar most. Of all fish and crustaceans there's nothing tastier than blue black *kamaron* and big fat *goramié*. Of all greens, the heart of palm is easily my favourite, while of all fruits, I adore the sweet and sour tang of wild *zanblon, franbwaz, prinn, zanbourzwa, mangasai and goyav-de-Chine* that you can pick straight from the trees.

Then my father took me hunting with him one day at the age of 11. At first we hunted just about everything: pheasant, partridge, hare, wild boar and deer. But when I shot my first buck at the age of 15, hunting deer became an all-consuming passion with me.

Most of the hunters in the country don't hunt alone. They band together in groups and go hunting regularly over the weekends during the hunting season from July to September. I used to hunt regularly with one group and at first enjoyed the *camaraderie* and conviviality that Mauritian deer-hunting is notorious for. But there was one thing we all took very seriously. That was the annual national competition to crown the hunter of the year who had bagged the largest buck of them all.

The Mauritian red stag is among the most beautiful antlered animal on the planet. Mature bucks usually weigh around 300 pounds, except for the largest among them, and they make some of the finest trophy animals in any hunter's collection.

Over the years I had harvested more bucks than any of the other hunters in my group. My ambition was not only to win the annual championship, I wanted to establish an all-time record.

The hunters in Mauritius came mostly from well-to-do families and included a rare breed belonging to the ultra exclusive super rich estate owners, descendants of the first French colonists who had settled on the island in the eighteenth century. These were established hunting dynasties who among themselves had bagged the island's largest stags averaging a height of 4 feet 6 inches and weighing up to 475 pounds, with an antler span of around 42 inches - a world class grade. It is widely believed that the Mauritian red deer that can grow antlers larger than that simply doesn't exist.

But despite well documented records of all the largest stags shot, their weight and the size of their antlers, the locations and the hunters who had shot them, unconfirmed stories continued to go round the hunting lodges about a huge stag, bigger than anything anybody had ever seen in their life, with enormous antlers measuring anything between 50 to 56 inches. He had been reported to have charged hunters who had dared violate his territory, who unfortunately didn't live to tell their tale. Forest dwellers called him the Monarch of the Forest.
Was he real? Did the Monarch really exist? Or was he made of the stuff that myth and folklore are made of?

From time to time, he was reported to have been spotted deep in the heart of the forest in the most rugged and inaccessible places. At times he was reported to have been spotted in two different locations at the same time!
When the more sceptical of my friends laughed the reports off as figments of the imagination, Suren, one of our more facetious companions, took them to task. But with Suren you can never tell when he's serious and when he's joking. It all depends on his mood.

50

'Why can't the Monarch be in two different places at the same time?' he asked.

'That can't be possible,' I said.

'Do you believe in God?' he countered.

'Yes I do,' I replied. 'What has God got to do with the Monarch?'

'It's like this,' he explained, 'most humans believe in God, yes, isn't that so? God, you will agree, doesn't exist for humans only. He exists for animals also, yes, isn't it so? Now God can appear in any place he wants. He can appear if he so wishes in different places at the same time, yes, isn't it so? Humans see God in human form, yes? Dogs also have a God, yes? You will agree that dog is closer to God in both sound and spelling, isn't it so? Deer too have their God in the form of deer. Maybe for a stag, God is a stag. If a human-looking God can appear in different places, why can't a stag-looking God appear in two different places, isn't it so, yes or no? I think we must not close our minds to the many possibilities of the natural world. Nature is magical, yes, isn't it so?

I found Suren's explanation logical and convincing, especially as I wanted very badly to believe that the Monarch really existed. Because by then, finding and shooting the Monarch had become a real obsession with me.

For me the traditional way hunting was organised in the country was only good for the exercise and *camaraderie*, but it was not as adventurous and challenging as I would have liked it to be. Hunters were stationed at various stands in the *chassé* (hunting ground) and beaters would 'beat' the deer out of the bush and force them to flee in the direction of the hunters for them to shoot.

It was as easy as that. But I loved deer hunting so much I never missed a single hunting party.

Then one day something happened that changed my life.

I was on my stand on the slope of a hill when I saw this beautiful doe leaping down the hill and running into some thick bush. I didn't have a clear view of her as she kept appearing and disappearing in the bush. I took aim and as soon as my crosshairs found her, I pulled the trigger. She buckled, staggered and fell. I knew I had only wounded her and that she would be trying to get away.

I ran up the slope to finish her.

As I broke from the thicket in which she had been moving, I saw her lying on her side, blood spurting from a big hole in her shoulder and reddening the grass. She was breathing painfully making a rasping guttural sound. Her two fawns were nestling over her, licking her wounds, trying to stop the flow of blood. When I approached her, she turned and fixed her eyes on me. How can I ever forget those large, sad, blood-soaked eyes? The pain and sadness I saw in them was so profound, I felt a chill pass all over my body and my hands began to shake.

She tried to get up, stumbled and fell. Again she tried, again she fell in a pool of her own blood, red patches darkening her brown coat and spreading on the grass. Her fawns kept clinging to her and were soaked in their mother's blood.

She could not move, she shook and twitched on the grass, agonising right there in front of her fawns, who were making moaning sounds and nudging her. She was going to die, and the least I could do was put her out of her pain.

I shot her in her heart. I could hear the thud of the bullet as it exploded her chest.

I couldn't leave the fawns alone in the wilderness. They would surely die if left on their own. I decided to take them home with me and release them in the forest when they were big enough to fend for themselves.

I've heard of hunters who had a similar experience, who as a result have stopped hunting altogether.

For weeks I was haunted by the doe's eyes and the infinite pain and sadness I had seen in them. Every time I thought of her, I felt sick and wanted to throw up.

Of all meats, I loved venison best. But after this experience, I stopped eating venison and all other red meats.

I kept away from hunting for one whole year during which I had plenty of time to think.

I began to see the forest not as a vast reserve where game animals are allowed to live and breed for hunters to shoot, but as an incomparable natural heritage, a wonderland to love and cherish for its own sake. I was thankful we still had a patch of forest left, and fearful that we might lose the last remnant of the magnificent rainforests that once covered our island. I began to see forest animals not as fair game but as creatures who had rights too and deserved to be treated better.

But hunting was in my genes and I couldn't keep away for long from the forest and all those friends that had been bonded to me by my lifelong passion.

In spite of myself, I found myself getting up early and meeting up with my hunting companions in the forest just as before.

But unknown to everybody, I loaded my rifle with a blank cartridge and kept a real bullet in my right pocket.

I went through all the motions of hunting. When I saw a good-sized buck, I took careful aim and fired, just as I used to do.

I am an experienced hunter and a dead shot with a hunting rifle. So when I fired and heard the loud detonation, I could almost hear the thud of my imaginary 'bullet' as it seared through flesh, bone, bristle and guts. But instead of dropping dead, the buck would stand erect for a nano second before bounding off to the safety of the bushes.

I thus had the double satisfaction of savouring the thrills of hunting and virtual 'killing', and also of seeing the buck bound off home to be with his kind.

But gradually, I began to distance myself from my hunting companions. The shooting orgy was too much and I couldn't bear to listen to the rifle shots reverberating across the woods, as the frightened deer raced for their life under a rain of bullets that followed them from glade to glade every time they broke from one shooting range to another. The poor deer never had a chance no matter how strong or how smart they were nor how fast they ran. All the odds were against them. All the hunter had to do was to settle himself comfortably at his station with a picnic hamper of sandwiches and drinks. And the deer would be driven towards him by dogs and beaters for him to shoot at. I couldn't feel I could justify the killing orgy in the name of sport.

I began to 'hunt' alone, armed with my trusted rifle loaded with a blank cartridge, and one real bullet I kept in my pocket.

I still hoped the Monarch really existed. This is why I always kept a real bullet in my pocket just in case I should one day chance upon him. I still dreamt of shooting him and pulverise all records past, present and future.

I told myself there was no contradiction in loving hunting but hating killing. I convinced myself that it was all right for me to go for the Monarch, who by that time must be an ancient patriarch well past his prime, who lived alone, far from his kind. It was better for him to fall honourably at the hands of someone who respected him, and have his magnificent antlers enshrined as a trophy for everybody to admire, rather than die in solitude and rot away in some lonely glen.

I interviewed all those who claimed they had seen him. I spent days and weeks walking and stalking on my own, reconnoitring the terrain where sightings had been made and learning all I could about him.

I learnt that until a few months back, the Monarch had been seen in the company of a doe, of an equally imposing size. But that for the last few months he had been sighted alone without the doe.

It was also reported that in the past, he had been sighted at different times of the day. But that for the last few months, no sightings of him in the mornings and early afternoons had been reported. All the sightings had been made in the late afternoons, one or two hours before sundown.

It wasn't difficult for me to put together a hypothesis in which many pieces of the puzzle fell into place. It was possible that there was not one, but two of these enormous red deer - the Monarch and his doe - who lived on their own far from the herd. This explains why he had been reported to have been seen in different places at the same time. In the past the Monarch had been sighted more often than not in the company of his doe.

55

Lately he had been sighted a few times, but he was always alone. It is possible that the doe had retreated to the heart of the forest to die in a place known only to them. The Monarch had stayed by her side and refused to leave her alone. This explains why he hadn't been seen during the day. He must have remained at the place where his doe had died and come out only at dusk to forage for food and to survey for a few minutes the wild and forested domain where he had lived his whole life and where he wanted to die.

I decided I would go for him even if I had to live in the forest for as long as it took. I began to walk and stalk every afternoon until the sun set. One afternoon as I was stalking the most difficult and rugged stretches of the forest where a forester had last claimed to have seen him, I picked up a spoor, a strong and distinctive one, that said that's my territory, keep out. I was intrigued and knew from the hoof marks that they were those of some unusually huge stag. I followed them in dense thickets deep into the woods, down ravines and up the steep slopes of wooded hills.

As the sun was going down on the western horizon and dusk was slowly advancing over the forest, I looked up and saw him climbing up the hill, moving ghostlike in the undergrowth, now appearing, now disappearing.
I followed him like a ghost too, from tree to thicket to boulder, soundless against the wind. I removed the blank cartridge and inserted the killer bullet into my rifle. I came as close as possible without rousing his suspicion. He was now standing on a rocky outcrop against the setting sun surveying his domain. Then he saw me.

He straightened to his full height and looked me directly in the eyes. Then, instead of charging me or running away, he stood still as if daring me to shoot. I took aim. He was in the crosshairs of my rifle. My finger was on the trigger.

He was awesome in his flaming fawn-coloured coat emblazoned by the colours of the setting sun. He was the most majestic creature I've ever seen. It would have been a sin to kill such a noble animal. I quietly removed the killer bullet, inserted the blank cartridge and fired.

***

THE STRUGGLE IS NEVER OVER

'When I saw oppression and ill-treatment, lawfully and unlawfully, I said to myself: I shall endeavour to change this one day.' Adolphe de Plevitz

The cane fields stretched all the way down from the slopes of the mountain to the distant coastline. Wavelets of steam rose shimmering from the piles of cut cane coating the labourers in syrupy sweat.

Suddenly a sickening scream tore through the sticky air striking fear in the hearts of the labourers who were cutting and loading the cane on bullock carts. They froze for a moment but quickly resumed their work as if they had heard nothing. Rama heard the scream and the machete that he held in his hand shook involuntarily as he tried to control the anger and revulsion that rose in his throat. He felt like vomiting but continued cutting the cane stalks with renewed vigour and frustration.

At night after the day's work, in his dark hut, he lay on his cot and allowed his mind to relive some episodes in his life that had brought him to this remote island thousands of miles from his native village in India.

THE INDIAN MUTINY

India, circa 1854-1857

Rama was about fifteen when the arrogance of the British began to create waves of unrest and frustration among the Indian population. Matters came to a head when Hindu and

58

Muslim *sepoys* (native soldiers) mutinied following rumours that their guns and bullets were greased with the fat of cows and pigs. In the wake of the mutiny, Rama's father joined the ranks of the revolutionaries who had taken up arms in an attempt to rid themselves of their British oppressors.

Rama followed his father's example and undertook many dangerous missions relaying instructions to the several insurgent leaders to get them to plan and coordinate their efforts.

However, after the initial successes, the revolution was ruthlessly crushed by the British with the help of thousands of native soldiers that formed the bulk of the British Indian army. Rama's father, Seewoodath, who had participated in the revolution, was wounded. He made his way to his village to see his wife and son. A traitor informed Captain Robert, the Commandant of the British troops garrisoned in the province, of Seewoodath's whereabouts. When the soldiers arrived in the village, Rama and his mother were coming back to their house accompanied by the *veyd* (native doctor).When they reached their house, Captain Robert and his men had already surrounded it and were ordering Seewoodath to come out with his hands raised. Seewoodath decided to fight to the death rather than surrender.

The soldiers set fire to the house to smoke him out. Rama's mother, Laxmi, rushed into the blazing house as a salvo of bullets hit Seewoodath in the chest. He dropped into Laxmi's arms and breathed his last. Laxmi stayed with her husband's body and let the fire consume them both.

Rama rushed into the blazing house to try and save his parents but he was held back by his uncles. He attacked the soldiers but was overpowered, cruelly beaten up and left unconscious. The soldiers also threatened to come back later to arrest him and lock him up, as attacking a soldier was considered a very serious crime. Captain Robert declared the village a nest of traitors and ordered the whole village to be razed to the ground. All those who had sympathised with the insurgents were dispossessed, their fields and property confiscated and redistributed to the loyal soldiers and all those who had secretly and openly sided with the British.

THE RECRUITING AGENT

When Rama recovered, he knew that he was a wanted man and could be arrested any time for treason and hanged. He went into hiding and decided he would leave India and start a new life elsewhere..

At the same time, Balessar Sahant, a recruiting agent, was actively contracting workers for a three-year period to work as indentured labourers in a country known as *Maricha,* located in the same ocean as India. Balessar was an expert at his job. He proceeded by inviting a few youths to the local *sharab khanna* (drinking house), got them toddy and some food and told them that there was an island called *Maricha*, not far in the Indian Ocean, that had been blessed by Lord Rama himself. Its streets were paved with gold; it was a land flowing with gold and honey, where they could find light work and high wages. He appealed also to their love of adventure and painted such a tantalizing picture of their life in *Maricha* that the youths were mesmerized and couldn't wait to sign up. They were taken to the Police Station and made to sign their work contract.

After three years on the run, Rama decided to join them and contract to work on the sugarcane plantations in Mauritius for a period of three years. He planned to keep a low profile and

60

return at the expiry of his contract period and start a new life in India.

The indentured workers were all assembled at the Depôt, on the banks of the river, in Calcutta, and after a few days, 350 workers were embarked on board the *Maharani* bound for Maricha Isand.

ON MONSIEUR LANDRU'S ESTATE

The conditions of work on Monsieur Landru's estate where Rama had been working for two years were far worse than he had been led to expect. Under the terms of their contract, the labourers had expected to be treated with reasonable decency and fairness. But it was clear that Monsieur Landru and many other planters didn't care about the labourers' rights and did pretty much as they wanted. The labourers were made to work like beasts of burden and were very often deprived of even their meagre salary and basic rations. Almost every day there were cases of brutal beatings, harassments, abuse and humiliations.

Tales of extreme cruelty from neighbouring villages often reached their ears, but instead of inciting them to take concerted action, they only strengthened their resolve to submit meekly to the planters' will. Rama had tried to persuade them to stand up and fight for their rights but apart from Fareed, a young labourer about his own age, all the other immigrants thought that any show of resistance would only invite more brutal punishment.

With the help of Fareed, Rama met some of the older labourers in secret one night and tried to rouse them from their apathy and resignation.

'Only last week,' he told them, 'a pregnant woman in the neighbouring village was shot dead. The guards had tied her husband to the wheel of the big mill and forced him to turn it. Every time he slowed down, they beat him until he lost consciousness. His wife pleaded with the planter to stop. The latter kicked her with his heavy boots and ordered his guards to continue with the punishment. She stood up and spat on his face. He took out his pistol and shot her at point blank.

'Why do they treat you worse than dogs?' he asked them. 'How long will you take things lying down? Why don't you do something about it?'

'The answer is simple,' he was told. 'Slaves do not ask questions.'

'No, this is not true. You have become slaves, because you don't ask questions,' Rama countered.

'It's easy for you to look down on us and think we are cowards. But you are wrong. Many labourers in the past have gone to the Protector of Immigrants and to the Police to complain about the way they were being treated. You know what happened to them. They were all arrested, beaten up, sentenced to pay heavy fines or be thrown in prison. And you know what happened to them when they came back. They were all cruelly punished. Some of them have never been heard of again. The truth is no one cares about us. Least of all the Protector of Immigrants and the Police. Greed has turned most of the planters into *rakshasas* (demons) who are sucking our blood.

'But there are signs that things will change. There is a White man, De Plevitz Saheb. He lives at Nouvelle Découverte near Long Mountain. People are saying that De Plevitz Saheb has sworn he will try and put a stop to our suffering. Those who dared to attend his meetings were brutally beaten up when they

62

came back to the village. The planters have ears and eyes everywhere.

We are not cowards. But it is foolish to act on our own without any support.'

But deep within their hearts, Rama knew, they were ashamed of themselves.

Rama and Fareed decided that they were going to do something, even if they died in the attempt. Anything, they reckoned, was better than doing nothing.

One Saturday evening, after their work, they slipped out of the village and walked all the way to Pamplemousses where De Plevitz was going to address some of the older immigrants who had finished their period of indenture, and were therefore free to work for the plantation owners or return to India.

'When you contracted to work in this country,' De Plevitz said, 'you had rights, and those rights were guaranteed you in your work contracts. You were guaranteed a regular salary, you were guaranteed essential rations and medical care. But when you came here, you found yourselves completely at the mercy of planters, many of whom treat you no better than slaves, and in many cases worse than slaves. When you go to the Protector of Immigrants and to the Police to complain, you are arrested, beaten up, sentenced to pay fines and very often imprisoned!

'Laws have been passed in this country, but these laws have been passed not to protect you, but to oppress you even more!

'Under the Pass system, the villages have become no better than prisons. You can't see the walls, but they are all around you. You can't travel a mile without being arrested as vagrants and imprisoned. The Police raid your homes at all hours of the day and night turning you out to see if your papers are in order.

Like the maroon hunts during the days of slavery, the Police organize vagrant hunts weekly, even on Sundays. They receive a percentage of the fines the so-called vagrants are sentenced to pay. Vagrant hunts have thus become a profitable source of income for a policeman. What kind of law is this that gives any ordinary policeman the right to arrest you whenever he feels like it, to beat you and lock you up, and to extort bribes from you?

'The system of Double Cut is even more oppressive. Planters can now mark a labourer sick or absent and cut two days' wages for every day he is marked absent. In some cases the poor labourer ends his period of indenture indebted to his employer. Nor can he return to India, because the return passage to India which was previously included in the terms of his contract has been abolished. He is therefore forced to reengage for a further period for a mere pittance.

'My friends, we cannot allow such injustices to continue any further. I am sure that if we act together, we can change all that. There are a few planters who treat their labourers with kindness and consideration. They are aware that it is the labourers who keep the wheels of their factories turning. They are aware that it is the labourers who are the real producers of wealth in this country. They deserve to be treated with dignity.

'Since you do not have anyone to represent you in the Government, the only way you can make your voice heard is by petitioning the Governor.

'I am therefore drafting a petition on your behalf. But to be valid, the petition must bear the signatures or the marks of at least 500 immigrants. The petition must also mention real cases of abuse and ill-treatment, and petitioners must be willing to come forward to substantiate the cases.'

'Unfortunately,' De Plevitz continued, 'so far very few immigrants have come forward to do so.' He appealed to those present to pass the word around and encourage the immigrants to come and meet him at his house at Nouvelle Découverte in Long Mountain.

When after the meeting Rama and Fareed reached their village in the early hours of the morning, they were immediately seized upon and brought to the compound of the sugar factory. Monsieur Landru arrived shortly afterwards.

'So you thought you could sneak out of the village and meet that traitor and live to poison the minds of the labourers?' he snarled. 'Do you seriously think that that traitor will succeed in his conspiracy against us? If I ever see him, I will shoot him like a dog.As for you, I'm going to make an example of you to show the labourers how we deal with dogs who dare defy us.'

At a signal from him, the guards seized Fareed and tied him to a loaded bullock cart. They then kept hitting him with heavy rattan canes forcing him to pull the cart round the factory. After some time, Fareed collapsed. The guards then dragged him and strung him upside down from a tamarind tree and took turns flogging him until he lost consciousness.

Rama could not bear it any longer. He leapt in front of Fareed's inanimate body, 'For God's sake,' he pleaded with the guards, 'please stop. I'll take his place. Beat me as much as you like but don't kill my friend!' He was quickly immobilised and the flogging continued until Fareed was dead.

Rama was then dragged before Monsieur Landru.

'So you are the dog that has been poisoning the minds of the labourers. I have saved you for something special. For starters, let's have some sport!'

At a signal from him, the guards brought out six ferocious dogs that were straining at their leashes growling and snapping their fangs viciously.

'These pitbulls haven't been fed since yesterday. They are very hungry and thirsty. When I order you to run, you better start running as fast as you can. I will then start counting. When I reach thirty, the guards will release the dogs. When they catch you, you would have wished you had never been born! Now start running for your miserable life, RUN!'

Contrary to expectations, Rama didn't run down the track leading to the canefields and the labourers' village. He turned around instead, clambered up the hilly and rock-strewn slopes behind the mill, then cut across the undergrowth towards the ravine at the bottom of which, the Grande Rivière Sud-Est roared its way to the sea. The dogs tried to chase him up the slopes but kept slipping and falling over each other. In their fury and confusion, they turned and attacked the guards.

'Get him and kill him!' Landru ordered. By the time the guards had recovered from their surprise and started chasing after him over the abrupt and wooded terrain, Rama had reached the ravine. He stopped there for a few seconds, said a prayer, then leapt into the roaring waters a hundred feet below.

A few days later a body was found at sea, mutilated and unrecognizable.

Mr Beyts, the Protector of Immigrants, didn't even bother to enquire into the incidents that had taken place on Monsieur Landru's estate. The Police officially declared that the immigrants on Monsieur Landru's estate had revolted and attacked the guards. One of them by the name of Fareed had died while resisting arrest. Another labourer by the name of Rama had drowned while attempting to escape.

Rama allowed himself to be swept out by the current to the open sea and then made his way under cover of darkness to a secluded stretch on the shore. He hid himself for a few days, coming out at night to hunt for food and inform himself of the latest news. He learnt that a dead body had been identified as being his and that he had been officially pronounced dead.

Rama had one thing on his mind. Go back and kill Landru. Avenge Fareed and all those whose blood Landru was sucking. He knew every nook and corner of the estate and the movements of the guards. He could easily sneak into Landru's house and overpower him. How he would love to see him on his knees, crawling and begging for his wretched life! How he would enjoy killing him slowly with his bare hands! He would then set fire to the house and sneak out as quietly as he had come. No one would suspect him. He was a dead man. And the dead are not accountable to the law.

But something within him held him back. Something within told him to put aside thoughts of revenge and use his freedom to help the immigrants get a fair deal for their sacrifices. He thought of De Plevitz. He had said he was going to fight for the rights and freedoms of the immigrants. Rama was convinced of his sincerity. As a bonded labourer, Rama's freedom of movement had been severely restricted. Every move he made, every word he said was reported to Landru. But as a dead man, he was free to move and act as long as he was not found out. Yes he could be more useful to De Plevitz 'dead' than alive.

ADOLPHE DE PLEVITZ

Under cover of darkness, Rama reached Nouvelle Découverte in the early hours of the morning. He knocked on the door of the wooden house in which De Plevitz lived. The door was opened by a tall and comely Creole woman, that Rama later learnt was Amélie, De Plevitz's wife. Rama told her he had walked all night and needed to see her husband. He was taken to the study and found himself face to face with De Plevitz. Rama was a tall and wiry young man, about 5 feet 11 with a swarthy complexion. He had a scar on his left cheek from a wound he had received during the Indian Mutiny. He found in front of him a man of about 33, equally tall and slim, with a scar from his left eyebrow to the middle of his forehead. Like Rama, his hair was dark and his eyes were brown. And both spoke English with a slight accent.

The two men sized each other up in silence for a few seconds. Both saw the same quiet determination in each other's eyes and knew instinctively that their meeting was not fortuitous. Rama told De Plevitz that he was officially presumed dead and he was prepared to lay down his life to help him in his fight to improve the plight of the Indian labourers.
De PLevitz told Rama that the time to take bold and decisive action had come. Governor Barkly had been succeeded by Arthur Hamilton-Gordon, who was known to be in favour of reforms of the labour laws in force in the country.

'I have drawn up a Petition to the Governor imploring him to look into the principal grievances the Indians suffer under the existing laws,' De Plevitz told Rama, 'and you could be of considerable help to me. I need someone from the ranks of the immigrants who would be able to get in and out of the villages and the estates without fear of the consequences to himself, someone without a name and without an identity, someone who could contact the labourers all over the country, set up cells on all the estates, and disappear without leaving any trace behind.'

De Plevitz asked Rama to help him collect as many signatures as possible and to encourage some of the labourers to come forward as witnesses to substantiate the cases mentioned in the Petition. It was a very dangerous mission. If he were caught, the planters would not hesitate to kill him. But Rama was ready to pay the price.

As the two men had to be constantly in touch to plan their moves and coordinate their efforts, it was agreed that to preserve his anonymity, Rama would alter his physical appearance and live on the estate as De Plevitz's aide.

Rama had first-hand experience of the brutal reprisals against labourers who dared to complain about their ill-treatment. He realized that witnesses could only come from among the Old Immigrants who had already served out their years of indenture and were no longer on sugar estates and therefore could not be subject to reprisals.

Rama travelled the length and breadth of the country carefully identifying and motivating the Old Immigrants. He set up cells and committees in many parts of the island and was able to persuade many not only to sign the petition but also to substantiate cases of abuse and violation.

De Plevitz, however, wasn't quite sure how he was going to go about collecting the signatures. At first he had invited the labourers to come to Nouvelle Découverte to sign the Petition. But the Inspector General of Police had threatened him with instant expulsion from the country if there was any trouble.

Rama knew that the Police was planning to use agitators to create trouble and find an excuse to get rid of De Plevitz. He therefore persuaded De Plevitz to carry the Petition round the districts and collect the signatures.

The response was beyond their wildest expectations. Old Immigrants were turning out in large numbers in support of the action undertaken by De Plevitz. On Tuesday 6 June 1871, the Petition with its 9,401 signatures or marks was presented to the Governor!

This was a great victory for De Plevitz and his supporters. But De Plevitz, always a man in a hurry, was not happy with the pace things were moving. He therefore increased pressure on the authorities by printing and circulating the Petition in the form of a Pamphlet which also included his comments and observations.

The reaction of the planters and the media was visceral. They clamoured for De Plevitz's immediate arrest for libel, and expulsion from the colony.
One newspaper publicly exhorted the planters 'to act to show that blood is necessary to wash away all the affronts which the colony has received from this wretched pamphleteer!'
From then on, De Plevitz was a marked man.

Rama now set himself the task of protecting De Plevitz every time he went to town or to any function where his presence was required. At the same time, putting to advantage his experience during the Indian Mutiny, Rama set up a network of young men around the country who would relay any information that might help anticipate and forestall any attempt on De Plevitz's life.

Rama thus learnt that the radical elements among the planters were led by Landru.

A meeting composed of persons in highly responsible positions was held on 18 August 1871 at which it was determined that De Plevitz should be publicly assaulted and abused to 'wash away' the affronts on the planting community. Lots were drawn as to who should strike the first blow. The lot fell to Mr Jules Lavoquer, and accordingly the latter, accompanied by a large number of friends and supporters, laid in wait for De Plevitz in Port Louis and gave him a severe beating. De Plevitz parried the blows as best he could, but sustained serious injuries to his body and head.

The Planters had planned to teach him a lesson but not to assassinate him. But unknown to them, a killer had been contracted by the extremist elements among them to take advantage of the confusion and stab De Plevitz to death. But the fates had decided otherwise.
Everything was going according to plan but before the contracted killer could strike De Plevitz dead, the police appeared on the scene and arrested both De Plevitz and Lavoquer and took them before the Police Magistrate. Lavoquer was released without bail while De Plevitz had to spend the night in police custody. Ironically, the overzealousness of the Police to arrest De Plevitz had saved his life!

This assault was followed by a succession of threats and intimidations. No action was taken by the Police, and, encouraged by the impunity of their actions, another meeting was held by the honourable members of the planting community at which it was resolved that on the day on which the case against De Plevitz was to be heard, a hired mob would attack and overturn his carriage as he came into town on his way to the Police Court. De Plevitz would then be dragged out and severely beaten, and if the police interfered they too would be attacked.

The extremist group, however, had met at Landru's house and decided that their members would take advantage of the situation and beat De Plevitz to death.

But for the second time, Providence intervened. As a result of information supplied by Rama's informers, the ridiculous charge against De Plevitz was dropped. This meant that he was not going to travel the next day to appear in court. The dropping of the charge against De Plevitz had thus thwarted the plan for the second attempt on his life!

Governor Arthur Hamilton-Gordon took a serious view of the degradation of law and order in the country under his administration. He issued a firm warning that he would not tolerate any further disturbance of good order and public peace and that the law would be rigorously enforced against all offenders.

The planters, realizing that their open defiance of the authorities and total disregard of the law was proving the very points that De Plevitz was making, decided to bide their time.

Infuriated at the turn of events, Landru decided to take matters into his own hands and rid the country once for all of De Plevitz. A few days later De Plevitz was on his way to the Pamplemousses court to appear in the case of an Old Immigrant charged with picking peas on his own land. De Plevitz's carriage was set upon on a deserted stretch of the road by Landru's accomplices and overturned. De Plevitz was violently projected from the carriage against a roadside tree and lost consciousness. Landru then emerged from behind the bushes and prepared to finish him off with his gun. Rama who had been travelling with De Plevitz quickly interposed himself between the killer and his victim brandishing a machete. When Landru saw Rama, he thought he was seeing a ghost. His finger shook on the trigger. In that split second, Rama hurled himself at him and with a mighty blow severed his jugular. As blood spurted from his neck, Landru fell forward, a horrified look on his face.

His accomplices, realizing what had happened, picked up his lifeless body and made off to his estate. After consulting the other members of their group, they decided that an official enquiry was to be avoided at all costs, as it would implicate their group in a criminal plot and embarrass the planting community in general. Landru was therefore declared to have been fatally wounded in a hunting accident.

On his part, Rama had thought it wiser not to tell De Plevitz about Landru's involvement in the attack. A police enquiry would not only blow his cover, it could seriously jeapardise the cause that they were serving. He therefore told De Plevitz that he had been able to put his assailants to flight.

As a result of De Plevitz's heroic crusade and the courageous mobilization of the Old Immigrants, a Royal Commission was at last appointed to inquire into the condition of the Indian labourers in Mauritius and to offer guidelines for future policy and legislation.

The Royal Commissioners, by careful and minute investigations proved that almost every statement contained in the Petition of the Old Indian Immigrants was well-founded, and in most cases strictly accurate.

The Royal Commission and its recommendations thus struck the first blow against the ruthless exploitation of Indian immigrants in Mauritius and shook the citadel of privilege to its very foundations.

EPILOGUE

When Governor Arthur Hamilton-Gordon left the colony, De Plevitz came under attack from every quarter, even from a quarter that he least suspected. He had exhausted all his financial resources and no longer had the means to support himself and his family. Rama and other close friends tried to raise funds but very few supporters came forward to help for fear of reprisals from the powerful planters who controlled all the banks and other economic resources of the country. De Plevitz had mortgaged his father-in-law's property and the banks refused to renew the mortgage unless he left Nouvelle Découverte. With his livelihood taken from him and credit universally refused him, De Plevitz had no option but to leave the island.

He would have liked to remain in the country and make sure that the Royal Commissioners' recommendations were put into practice. That was not going to be. But he had the satisfaction of having accomplished the most important part of his mission and was confident that Rama and others from among the labourers themselves would complete the task he had set himself.

On Sunday, 23 April 1876, Adolphe de Plevitz boarded the ship *Capella* bound for Sydney and a new life. He had almost no
74

possessions with him except a few articles of clothing, some letters and papers. As he stood on the deck of the ship and watched the receding shoreline of the country in whose service he had sacrificed everything - his time and energy, his wife and children, his friends and relatives - he remained undaunted to the very end.

'I am leaving this country,' he promised himself, 'to continue the fight against oppression and injustice in other parts of the world wherever Fate takes me. The struggle is never over.'

It was only a century after De Plevitz left Mauritius that the first official recognition was given to his struggle, when in 1977, the Municipal Council of Port Louis unanimously approved the motion of a young Councillor, Rama Poonoosamy, to name a street in the capital after Adolphe De Plevitz, one of the bravest freedom fighters in the history of Mauritius.

After De Plevitz's departure, Rama decided that the best way he could continue the fight for the rights and freedoms of the labourers was by imparting the benefits of education to their children, both boys and girls, so that they could participate fully in the making of a country they had made their own. He toured the country tirelessly encouraging parents to send their children to school. Eventually leaders emerged from among their own ranks to continue the fight from generation to generation to help build on this land of immigration a country that everyone can call their own and where no one is more equal than others.

Rama represents all those unsung heroes who have selflessly served this country and its people, as against all those who have shamelessly used this country and its people to serve themselves.

***

THE MINISTER AND THE ARTIST

Like a new broom the newly appointed Minister of Arts and Culture was determined to sweep the cultural scene of the island clean and turn it into a nursery of innovation and creativity. For too long, succeeding Governments had baulked at tampering with the multi-ethnic, multi-cultural, multi-religious and multi-lingual heritage of the people of our rainbow nation. At all 'national' celebrations, Mauritians were, year in year out, served a stale succession of Hindi, Urdu, Tamil, Telugu, Mandarin, Creole, Bhojpuri, English, French and Rodriguan cultural programmes. And God help the hapless Minister if any of the diverse cultural components of our rainbow nation felt *lésé* (aggrieved).

But our newly-appointed Minister of Arts and Culture was determined that this time around he could make a difference. Thirty years into Independence, a new generation of artists were struggling to forge a new cultural identity, enriched and not constrained by our multicultural diversity. He was going to give voice to their aspirations and *faire de notre musique, la voix de notre île* (make of our music the voice of our island). He was searching for a musical expression inspired by the rich diversity of musical traditions in the country that would be reckoned a unique contribution to the world's musical heritage. The Mauritian was *un enfant de mille races* (a multi-ethnic child), and was destined to become the prototype *de l'homme universel* (the universal man); and Mauritius, he affirmed, located as it is at the crossroads of the world's great cultures and civilisations, was destined to become *une île phare* (a beacon) showing the way to the future.

The Minister was keenly aware, however, that this wasn't going to be easy. In the first place, the Ministry of Arts and Culture was the Cinderella of the Government's priorities, its budget barely sufficient to cover the salaries of its officials and the costs of the numerous mandatory annual celebrations. To make matters worse, while people paid lip-service to innovation and change, there was, in the population in general, and the old guard in particular, a deep-seated suspicion of all change and innovation.

And so it happened that while the Minister was on a visit to India, he was invited to a concert by Bryan D'Silva, a brilliant pianist who, within the space of nine months, had taken Mumbai by storm. Bryan D'Silva was unique among great Indian artists in that he played Indian tunes and compositions on the piano, a distinctly western instrument. East and West met in his music and the effect was mesmerising.

The Minister was even more interested when he learnt that Bryan D'Silva came from Goa, the smallest state of India, that, like Mauritius, was gifted with beautiful golden beaches and a friendly people who were exposed to a great variety of cultural traditions and who lived in a state of permanent cultural osmosis. The Minister saw in Bryan D'Silva the catalyst that would help bring about greater intercultural sharing and musical fusion in the island.
He lost no time sharing his dreams with Bryan D'Silva and succeeded in persuading him to come to Mauritius as his guest

on the occasion of the National Day celebrations that were to take place the following month.

The Minister had chosen a cinema hall in his rural constituency as the venue for the sole concert Bryan D'Silva was giving. The general public was invited and admission was free. The choice of Bryan D'Silva, a pianist, rather than a popular Bollywood star as the Minister's special guest, had raised a few eyebrows. But to the initiated, it was one concert they could not afford to miss, and they drove from long distances to see the maestro live in action.

Crowds of festive people of all ages and cultural backgrounds were coming in droves from all over the constituency in buses freely provided by individual operators, packing the theatre to capacity, spilling out onto the aisles, the foyer and even outside the cinema hall. Ministry officials had turned out in full force and were desperately trying to keep things under control. Finally, with the help of the Police (dressed for the most part in civilian clothing), a semblance of order was restored and the show could begin.

The local band at the back of the stage struck up a fanfare of sorts and the Minister, accompanied by Bryan D'Silva, took up their position front centre-stage. The band then played the Indian national anthem followed immediately by the Mauritian *Motherland*. When other formalities were completed the Minister in his welcome address shared his dream and his vision with the audience.

'Our renowned guest,' the Minister said, 'comes from a state in India, which is similar to our own country in many respects. He has experimented with a large variety of genres and musical

78

expressions. He has succeeded in developing a sound and a style that are unique. I firmly believe that our musicians will gain a lot by following his example.

'Ladies and Gentlemen, respected mothers and sisters, my young friends, my dear little children,' the Minister concluded, 'I have very great pleasure in giving you the man whose voice is in his fingers, and when his fingers touch the piano, the piano sings. Ladies and gentlemen, put your hands together to welcome the maestro who makes the piano sing!'

The Minister then left the stage and took up his seat in the front row of the theatre among other Ministers and dignitaries.

Bryan D'Silva thanked the Minister and the audience for their very warm welcome and said he was ready to begin.

Three Ministry officials briskly walked up to the centre of the stage, where they installed a Yamaha electronic synthesiser on a stand. After testing and fine-tuning the sound, Lampataw, the senior technician, told Bryan D'Silva he could begin. Bryan D'Silva could not quite understand what was going on. He had already noticed the absence of a piano on the stage, but had thought that at the right moment, a piano would surely be wheeled in. When he realised that instead of a grand piano, he was expected to play a Yamaha synthesiser, he went all red in the face and felt his feet buckling from under him.

'You expect me to play this ...er... instrument!' he stammered in disbelief.

'Begging your pardon, Sir,' Lampataw, the senior technician, blurted out in an offended tone, 'this instrument, as you call it, is a PSR S950 top of the range Yamaha Portatone synthesiser. It plays different styles in different voices and numerous variations. It is also equipped with a full range of bass and rhythmic accompaniments. It has pitch control options, and is fitted out with an oscillator and a DJ pattern. Begging your pardon, Sir, this instrument, as you call it, is an all-in-one orchestra!'

'But I don't play the synthesiser. I play the piano,' Bryan D'Silva protested angrily.

'Piano! Who plays the piano nowadays? Begging your pardon, Sir, I assure you this synthesiser is the most versatile instrument going round these days. This little marvel is the mother of all musical instruments. The world's greatest groups play it - Santana, Sting, Nirvana, Wine and Roses and all the rest of them. Let me show you. You just press this button, and it becomes a piano. It's as easy as that. Even a child can play it!'

Lampataw then struck the opening notes of *Au Clair de la Lune.*

'Just listen to this. It plays the piano better than a piano! Now listen to the same tune played on the clarinet.'
Lampataw then pressed another button.
'What do you have to say to this? Begging your pardon, Sir, this instrument is a state of the art technological marvel!'

Bryan D'Silva kept looking at the instrument with mounting disbelief and consternation.
'You play the piano,' Lampataw said dismissively, 'well then just press this button and bang away!'

Bryan D'Silva did not know whether to laugh or cry. He was still in shock when a panic-stricken Minister rushed onstage to try and salvage his political future from certain collapse. By espousing progressive ideas and championing unpopular causes, the Minister had become an easy target for the Opposition and an embarrassment to his own Party. But instead of taking the easy way out, he had stuck to his principles and managed to confound friends and foes alike. But this time he knew that ridicule, more powerful than friends' betrayal and enemies' stratagems, was going to be his undoing. But like most politicians, survival instincts were built into his genes. The audience was rocking with laughter thinking it was all a joke and formed part of the entertainment programme. The Minister decided to do some damage control by playing for time.

'My dear countrymen,' he told the audience, 'I've forgotten to mention something that you will be very glad to hear. As you all know, Bryan D'Silva is a living legend in India. When I met him there, he told me he had heard about our beautiful rainbow country and had been very much impressed by our artists and musicians. He had always dreamt of coming to our country one day to listen to our multicultural voices. He insisted that he would play for us only after we sing and play for him. Ladies and Gentlemen, can we make his dream come true? Yes, Yes, Yes We Can! Can we play *radio-krosé* (a song contest)? Yes, Yes, Yes We Can!
Thank you, Ladies and Gentlemen, thank you for your overwhelming response. For my part, I shall be only too happy to give a cash prize of Rs 500 to the top three participants who win the audience's favours.'

The Minister detailed a Ministry official to take over as anchor while he whisked Bryan D'Silva away backstage where he studied his next moves. He learnt that there were only three grand pianos in working order on the whole island, two belonging to two five-star Beach Hotels, and the third one located in the Conservatoire François Mitterrand, donated by the French Government. He immediately called the Director of the Conservatoire, coaxing, cajoling and threatening her into loaning the grand piano for that evening against a blanket approval of her proposed plans for building and equipping a new wing of the Conservatoire.

While hectic behind-the-scenes arrangements were being made, the *radio-krosé* was proving to be a huge success. The theatre was reverberating with the cheers and jeers, the hoots and toots of the audience.

The *radio-krosé* had quickly escalated into an all-out contest among the principal musical groups in the Minister's constituency, hell-bent on walking away with the Rs 25,000 cash prize the Minister had later laid out to spice up the evening's entertainment.

It was well over two hours into the programme when the grand piano made its appearance. By that time, those of Bryan D'Silva's fans who had travelled long distances had given up all hope of seeing their idol perform live and had all left. I had no choice but to leave with my friends, but instead of feeling disappointed and bitter, we had found the whole experience so funny and bizarre that we rocked with laughter all the way back home. This was one of the stories, we told ourselves, we would never tire of telling our friends and our children. Too bad if the joke was at the expense of our own countrymen, and of our own Minister of Arts and Culture of all people!

Back in the cinema hall, the Minister had a difficult time placating the over-excited crowd. There were four groups that were fighting it out to the bitter finish; two were sega groups and two were Bhojpuri groups. The excitement had reached fever pitch with excited fans cheering wildly for their favourite groups. Neither the anchor nor the jury were willing to come up with a verdict. They were only too well aware that any verdict in favour of one group or another could spell big trouble. It is only after the Minister had proclaimed all the four groups *ex aequo* winners, and invited them to come the following week to collect their prizes at the Ministry in Port Louis, that Bryan D'Silva was finally able to begin.

I must confess that as I had left earlier, I can't pretend to know how the evening progressed. Did Bryan D'Silva succeed in casting his spell and winning over the over-excited audience? Did the Minister succeed in averting a monumental 'fiasco' and saving his political future? All these are questions that are better left to the reader to puzzle out.

***

LETTER TO MY BELOVED

If this letter is in your hands and you are reading it, it means that the story it is about to tell was meant to be told. For no one in the world apart from me knows of its existence, not even the person to whom it is addressed.

By the time you read its contents I shall be no more. But before crossing over to that unknown shore, a force that could not be withstood impelled me to confide in this letter fragments of my life, which I then placed in this bottle, the very same bottle from which I had poured out our drinks the very first time Carlos came to my apartment at 20 St George Square, on that rain-soaked night on Saturday 23 December, 1964.

I then climbed to the top of the cliff in whose shadow I have been living these past few years and threw the bottle out into the sea. The Ocean will decide whether our story will live, or whether it will accompany me to the grave.

My Dearest Carlos,

Exactly thirty years today, on Saturday 23 March, I saw you for the very first time as you were awkwardly picking your way in the sanctified chapel of our Blessed Lady of Carmel, Oxford, where I was delivering the first of a series of talks on St John of the Cross and other Catholic mystics. When our eyes met and mine held yours, I forgot where I was and kept looking at you until you were finally seated, not without treading on someone's toes, tripping and sending your notebooks flying in all directions.

All this must have taken maybe one minute or two, but for me time had stopped, my eyes could see only you. Like the lenses of a camera, my eyes zoomed in on you bringing you closer and closer until I could clearly see the contours of your face, until I could even see that you had not buttoned up your black graduate gown properly, until I could even smell the fragrance of your body.

After my talk, I rushed through the accolades of the enraptured throng to meet you. But you were gone.
I didn't know your name, nor where you came from. I could see you were not from the UK, nor Europe or America, nor Africa, not even Asia. You were not from any of the places I knew, but there was something of all these places in you, in your expressions, in your gait, in your looks. Your face had the mystique of the East, set in the features of a Michelangelo's honey-complexioned David.
During the weeks that followed, I could think only of you. I found myself calling you *Carlos! Carlitos! Carlite!* I started looking for you everywhere.

One evening, amidst the usual high spirits and convivial buzz that precede dinner in the College Hall, I sighted you in the company of Sister Constancia, a Carmelite nun who was a friend of mine. It seemed that you had materialised all of a sudden from nowhere in answer to my prayers. I walked straight to you and while Sister was introducing us, I found it most natural to embrace you like a friend I was meeting after a long time although you were many years younger than me. We decided to meet the next day for tea and continue our discussions about eastern and western mysticism.

At first we met on weekday afternoons for tea, then we met regularly for lunch, and soon we decided to work seated next to each other at the Bodleian where I helped you with your research.

SATURDAY 23 DECEMBER 1964

We had become used to meeting every Saturday evening after my talk to one of the many fraternities in Oxford, and eating out at a quiet and cosy restaurant very close to my lodgings. After the meal you used to see me off to my door before returning to the Commonwealth Students Club where you were lodging. One Sunday evening, I was giving a special lecture on the anniversary of St John of the Cross attended by some important visiting church dignitaries and theologians. I had also told you how much I wanted you to come to the lecture.

It was one of the most emotional lectures I had ever given. The large attendance in that gothic cathedral seemed to hang on every word I said and I had to pause several times when I was describing the Dark Night of the Soul of St John of the Cross, as many tender souls in the audience could not restrain their tears and were sobbing uncontrollably. From the elevated rostrum where I stood, I could zoom in on you and my heart cried out when I saw tears streaming down your cheeks. That evening, I noticed a marked change in the way you looked at me and in the way you addressed me. Your eyes were moist for the most part of our dinner together. Gone were your light-hearted and irreverent banter. You reminded me more of a pilgrim soul who had been bequeathed a glimpse of his heart's desire.

After dinner, as we were approaching my lodgings, we were caught in a sudden downpour and were thoroughly doused. I insisted that you dry yourself at my place before going to your hostel.

I helped you remove your clothes and get into one of my favourite Japanese dressing gowns which I had named the 'robe of a million stitches', because of the myriads of intricate and minute hand-embroidered patterns on a golden satin kimono. I poured out for you in a chiselled cup a rare liqueur that had been gifted me by a Carthusian monk, and seated you on my large rocking chair in front of the hearth where a glowing fire was already burning sending warm gules over your reclining body in the dimly lit room.

As the hot liquor burnt down your throat, I could see your body buckle taut as an arc, then gradually settle down languorously in the armchair while an unfathomable expression played in your eyes and around your lips. You looked like a reclining David and I pictured Michelangelo kneeling in adoration before him. I knelt down in adoration at your feet and after gazing up lovingly at you I placed my head on your lap.

I could feel your fingers playing softly with my hair and gently stroking the back of my neck. I dared not speak, nor move nor breathe. I wanted that moment to last forever. I lost consciousness of my own self and of you and of everything around us and passed into an ecstatic state where I had become one with you, and you had become one with me.

After you left that night, I spent the night in prayer and meditation. In the morning I went to early mass and took communion. I had great faith in the selfless love I bore you, in its purity. Now that we had been meeting for six months almost daily, I had religiously kept away from any physical closeness with you. Although I was dying to embrace you and pour out my love, I didn't dare invite you to my apartment. I would have given everything to hold you in my arms. But my fear of losing you was stronger than my yearning for you.

The next day, you didn't come to the Bodleian. As it had become my wont, I had placed all the books you had requisitioned on your study desk, and I waited for your familiar steps. It was now past lunch time and still you hadn't come. I could imagine what was going on in your mind. Above all I feared an emotional backlash that could inflict irreparable damage on our relationship and drive you away from me. You were so innocent, so trusting, so generous and so sensitive. But I knew that you came from an orthodox background and that you had grown up in a society where close physical relationships between two men were taboo. I began to fear the worst.

My first reaction was to rush to your hostel and find out why you hadn't come to the Bodleian as was our daily routine. But I thought it was better to let you come to terms with what had happened and give you time to get over any negative emotions that you might associate with the new turn in our relationship.

The following day, as was my custom, I went to church to attend early mass and to take communion. I took the priest aside and told him I wanted him to hear my confession. The father heard me pour out my love and my fear in silence. When I had finished, he told me he understood my pain and my distress. He told me that if my actions were motivated by love, I need not fear. He told me to pray and to have faith in God's compassion. That our Father is a loving father, that he understands every beat of my human heart. He told me I had to be sure that above

88

all I cared for you and your feelings, to forget myself and not do anything that might hurt you.

I then went to the Bodleian, took my seat at my customary place, and waited for your footsteps. 9.30 a.m., you had not come; 10.30, there was no sign of you;11.30, nothing. I could bear it no longer. I had stopped thinking. My mind was in a whirl. Without realising what I was doing, I found myself rushing out of the Bodleian and propelled to your hostel. I kept believing I would succeed in getting you to understand that you need not be ashamed of my love for you nor of your love for me.

When I reached your hostel, the receptionist told me that you had vacated your room and had left for an unknown destination. He told me that you had left no forwarding address. He then gave me a letter addressed to me.

I took the letter from his hands in a daze and went out in the park adjoining your hostel and sat down on a bench. My hands were shaking as I opened the letter and began to read:

'Dearest Julio,
Please excuse me for leaving so suddenly. But that was the only course open to me. I could no longer stay in the same town as you, after last night.
When I met you six months ago, I was not sure about many things. But there was one thing I knew I wanted to do. I knew that after my 'peregrinations' in the countries of the West, I was going home to my country where I belong. Until then, I would keep all the windows of my mind open and let all the cultures of all lands to be blown about as freely as possible without allowing myself, however, to be blown off my feet by any.

I was therefore open to all kinds of experiences as part of my education. It was in this frame of mind that I met you. I know you think I'm a very innocent island boy uncorrupted by the ways of the world. The truth is I am far more worldly wise than you think. But you didn't want to see me as I am. You wanted to see in me a virginal young man from some remote island that you had 'discovered' and wanted to wean and nurture. You wanted to be my guide, my mentor, my protector, and eventually, my lover. Before I met you, I was happy doing the things I'm best at. I met the people I felt most at home with and did the things that most young people of my age love doing. You introduced me to a world where I met people I would never have known in my life - famous authors, poets, musicians, composers, artists, scholars and philosophers, mystics and theologians. I began to think that there was a special Providence that was shaping my life in spite of myself, and I just allowed myself to flow with the current.

At first you seemed too good to be true. But your overwhelming love for me soon overcame my doubts and hesitations. I came to trust you unreservedly. I really felt you were an angel that a special God had sent to enlighten me, to guide me, to inspire me. I didn't feel you were like any other mortal I have known. You really are not of this world. I can't tell you how happy you have made me and how much I have prized our friendship. But I did suspect after some time that your love for me was not entirely angelic.

You remember in order to help me discover what I wanted to do after my studies, you invited me, in your capacity as President of a Pan-American Peace Organisation, to come to your country as a Visiting Fellow and visit American universities for one year at the end of which I was free to decide whether to accept a job with any institution of Higher Education of my choice, or to return to my country. I was aware you had wanted to reassure me with this amazing offer that you wanted me to exercise total freedom in my choice of a career and country of residence, and not feel bound to you for the rest of my life.

Dearest Julio, I appreciate your solicitude but I could never live in a country where I was only a visitor, a guest, a second class citizen. In my country I am at home everywhere, in a humble fisherman's hut, in a simple labourer's cottage as well as in the residences of the rich and powerful. I was only casting anchor awhile in your world. But I knew that sooner or later I would have to go home where I belong, where I am needed and where I would find meaning in my life.

I admired your self-imposed restraint and wondered how long you would be able to hold out. I sensed how much you wanted to hold me in your arms and allow yourself to be devoured by your all-consuming passion. I was wondering when you were going to take the next step. You see, dearest Julio, I'm not half as innocent as I look. I knew I had all the cards in my hand and was waiting for the conflagration to happen. And when it did happen, it caught me completely by surprise.

All these years I have been away from my country, I had plenty of time to free myself from the small island mentality and all its prejudices and to follow my own inclinations. I had an exciting time discovering the real me and finding my own path in life. I have always felt I was the hunter, the explorer, the discoverer, the doer. I welcomed the bitter-sweet taste of self-discovery, and the beguiling thrills of conquest.

Last night, while you reclined at my feet, I was thrilled at the thought of 'possessing' such a one as you. You said nothing, but in your eyes, tears were smiling. All I could see was your desire, your adoration, and the depth of your need for me. And instead of feeling the thrills of conquest, I felt for the first time in my life, the joys of total surrender, of giving and not counting. I was overjoyed in being the object of so much love and the source of so much happiness. My surrender to you was at the same time a great triumph over myself.

When I woke up this morning, I relived the moments we had spent together and I was filled with doubts and misgivings. The conditioning of a lifetime came back to taunt me. I was lost and completely confused. I would have given both my arms to be the person you expect me to be. I would have loved to love you the way you love me. But I am not made of the same stuff as you. I am the way I am and I cannot change that. What is more, I am proud of being what I am. I cannot be the person you want me to be. When I met you, I thought it was all in the scheme of things; and that when I go back to my country, I would be more prepared to meet the challenges ahead of me.

You have filled my soul with wonder and awe. For the first time in my life, I have come as close as possible to those rare spirits that come to this world once in a long while. But although I understand with my mind and my heart that two adults may choose to love and cherish each other, my whole body is repelled at the very thought of physical intimacy between two persons of the same sex. I must confess I was swept off my feet last night and I am not sure I'm proud of what happened. I feel that in my search of knowledge and wisdom, I have taken a wrong turn. I have been lingering too long in a world in which I do not belong. The time has come for me to return to my country before I cross the point of no return. I have no choice but to leave you and think of you as a wonderful dream from which I have been rudely awakened. I am leaving this town and resuming my journey. Please do not look for me. Let me tread the road that I think Destiny has charted out for me. We belong to two different worlds; we have to go our separate ways.'

Like a man walking in his sleep, I went and sat down by the river Isis, and cried my heart out. I was completely devastated. Although I was certain I hadn't done anything wrong, I was keenly aware of the torment that you must have been going through. For weeks and months afterwards I was torn by the overwhelming urge to find you and plead with you to continue our friendship on your terms and without any strings attached. But a voice deep within told me I had no right to hurt you, I had no right to transplant you to a world which was so much alien to your own deep-rooted culture and values.

I spent many weeks and months in prayer and meditation. I was keenly aware that I was going through my Dark Night of the Soul. God was testing me. I had no right to fail Him. I had no right to succumb to my own desires. It was my ordeal by fire, I kept telling myself; the fire was meant to burn off the impurities in my soul. But the road back to sanity was long and arduous and I was walking it alone.

But I had not lost you. You were always with me. You were my inspiration, my song. You remained in my thoughts, in my body, in my soul. You had become part of me.

I threw myself into my work as an ambassador of peace like a drowning man clutching at a straw. I wrote many books and became rich and famous. But in the solitude of the night, my body ached for you, my soul cried out for you, and I called your name like a beadsman telling his beads: *'Carlos! Carlos! Carlitos! Carlite!'*

Many years later, I was travelling on a yacht with a few friends. Without any prompting from me, they decided to stopover for one day and one night in the harbour of your capital city Port Louis. You know I do not believe in coincidence. Everything has a place in the cosmic play of which we are a part. The moment I arrived in your country, all I could think of was you. I found myself enquiring after the place where you were born and grew up, and whose address I knew by heart.

I called a cab, and asked the driver to take me somewhere near the address which had been indelibly etched on my mind – *11, Ave des Bengalis, Quartier des Bougainvillées, Port Louis*. I swore to myself that I would only walk down the street where you had lived, look at the mountain which you had often climbed as a child, walk past the house in which you had spent your childhood, and, should I by a thousand to one chance happen to see you, I would hide somewhere and watch you from a distance and under no circumstance approach you.

How my heart pounded as I stepped on the cobbled street where you had lived. Like someone in a dream, I walked past the large wooden gate of *11, Ave des Bengalis*. After walking up and down the street a few times, I found myself stopping in front of the gate. I found my hand pressing the bell. I rang once, then twice, and waited, dying to see you, but praying at the same time that you wouldn't be in. After a long moment when the world stood still, a young man opened the door. He was an image of the Carlos I had first met in Oxford so many years ago!

When I saw him, my heart started pounding uncontrollably against my ribs. I felt dizzy and had to lean against the young man for support. He sensed I was not feeling well and supported me for a while. I was sweating profusely and my hands were shaking and my voice sounded as if it was coming from somewhere far away.

I told him I was all right and asked him if this was your house. He had a curious look in his eyes, as if I reminded him of someone he knew or had been told about, and he was figuring out who he could be.

'My father is not at home,' he replied. 'Is there anything I can do for you?'

I told him I was a friend of one of his father's friends, and I had been asked to enquire after him.

Young Carlos told me his father was giving the first of a series of talks on the Spiritual Quest at an Interreligious Conference of spiritual seekers at the Carmelite Monastery, Vacoas, and that I would find him there if I wanted to meet him.

I had the taxi take me to Vacoas. When I arrived there, I entered the portals of the Monastery and positioned myself behind one of the pillars where I could remain unseen and have a clear view of you and also hear your every word.

How can I describe the state I was in? I gazed and gazed at your adored face not even daring to blink an eye. I drank you with my eyes and felt your words echoing in my ears the essence of our discussions during our long walks across the verdant parks of Oxford, along the banks of the Isis, at tea time. I felt that even if the words came from your mouth, it was I who was speaking through you.

'In the Spiritual Canticle,' you were saying, 'St John of the Cross uses an allegory: the search of the beloved husband by his wife. The wife feels herself wounded by love, and this makes her to start the search for the Beloved; the wife asks everywhere for her beloved in despair until husband and wife are finally reunited.

In the same way, a spiritual seeker is one who has been wounded and can find no rest until he or she is reunited with God.

'I am concluding my talk today,' you said, 'with the opening verses from the Spiritual Canticle of St. John of the Cross that my mentor in Oxford loved to recite when he spoke about the spiritual quest:

Where have You hidden,
Beloved, and left me moaning?
You fled like the stag
After wounding me;
I went out calling You, and You were gone.
O shepherds, you who go
Through the sheepcots up the hill,
If you shall see Him
Whom I love the most,
Tell Him I languish, suffer, and die.
In search of my Love
I will go over mountains and strands;
I will gather no flowers,
I will fear no wild beasts;
And pass by the mighty and the frontiers.

O groves and thickets
Planted by the hand of the Beloved;

96

O verdant meads
Enamelled with flowers,
Tell me, has He passed by you?

'In my subsequent talks,' Carlos was saying, 'we will see how once the desire to seek out the Beloved has been aroused in the Seeker, how he will discover gradually that that for which he has longed for has always been with him and within him. The Beloved could be physically thousands of miles away, on the other side of the world, or even on the other side of heaven, yet in truth, he has never been farther than the Seeker's very breath. Thus the Seeker and God, like the Bride and Bridegroom, like the Lover and the Beloved, have always been one.'

When Carlos ended, there was a long silence heavy with tears that were freely streaming from the eyes of many of the young seekers in the audience. Then the applause followed, long and sustained.

I felt I was living a wonderful dream that God in His mercy had vouchsafed me. I found that I was leaning heavily for support against the pillar which had concealed me from Carlos's vision. I knew I had to get away before my feet grew too weak to carry me. By a great effort of will, I tore myself away from the pillar, and reeled my way as best I could through the portals back to the taxi that was waiting for me.

When I was back on board the yacht, I locked myself in my cabin and prostrated myself before God who in His great mercy had granted me this ultimate boon. I felt blessed beyond the wealth of kings and blessed also to know that Carlos had also welcomed me into his heart as a blessing from God.

***

JONAH

Jonah had earned a place in a 5-star secondary college by ranking among the 300 top Certificate of Primary Education (CPE) candidates, but had discovered early in his second year that the things that interested him most interested his teachers least. In class his mind and his imagination kept wandering away from the white board, outside the walls of the classroom, away from the precincts of the college to focus on the things he loved doing.

And the things he loved doing were many and varied. He loved cats and dogs and loved looking and caring after them. He loved plants and trees and flowers and enjoyed looking and caring after them. He self-taught himself, with the help of the internet, a number of creative skills. He became so good at these that over the weekends he was regularly invited to participate in youth rallies and teach young people of his age the things he was good at.

By the time he was in Form 4, he had lost all interest in 'academic' studies. There was one particular teacher that he disliked. The latter had an autocratic style of teaching. He never taught. He just talked for thirty to forty minutes solid after which he set homework. When he was in the mood, he told stories in which he was always the hero. He used his class as a convenient platform to launch on his ego trips. But Jonah was a prickly customer and liked pricking the teacher's ego balloon, much to the raucous appreciation of the class.

This is how Jonah started getting into trouble. He started spending time in detention for disrupting the class and for not doing his homework. He started shirking classes and got involved in fights with two bullies who were constantly harassing him.

Jonah was essentially a non-violent person who abhorred the use of force. When he was a child, his brother Zayn, one year his senior, could not stand his constant jabbering and often kicked him. His brother Izra, two years younger than him, followed Zayn's example, and between them they gave him a bad time. When Izra bullied him and called him *enn poul mouyé* (a coward), he never retaliated.

I was angry with him.

'Jonah, why do you let Izra bully you and you do nothing about it? He thinks you are a "*poul mouyé*". He's as skinny as a *bomli sek* (dried bombay duck) and you're twice his size. You could knock him out anytime. Go on, show him you're not a *poul mouyé*. Hit him, and that'll shut him up for good.'

Jonah said nothing and endured Izra's bullying in silence.

One day I told him he should not allow Izra or anybody else for that matter to call him names and humiliate him. I told him he was much stronger than Izra. Why do you allow him to bully you? Why don't you teach him a lesson? Are you afraid of Izra? Are you scared of fighting? Are you a coward?. Come on what is it?

'You know grandpa, Izra is my little brother. I don't want to hit him. I'm scared I might hurt him bad.'

'But Jonah,' I said, 'what about school? Do you let other boys bully you and you keep quiet?'

Jonah said he preferred to avoid them.

When he was in Form 4 Jonah shot up. He grew tall, muscular and strong for his age.

One day while he was relaxing on the 'hill', a wooded knoll on the school precincts, the two bullies who had been constantly harassing him in Form 3 attacked him. He was forced to defend himself. He came out of the fight with broken lips and many bruises, but his tormentors had to be taken to hospital for treatment.

As a result he was suspended from school for one week and the list of his wrongdoings grew longer.

On two other occasions, he was caught smoking cigarettes with two other blacklisted friends of his. As if that was not bad enough, there were dark rumours of students smoking marijuana on college premises. The college was on red alert.

Jonah and his two buddies were labelled 'problem students' and whenever there was some wrongdoing at the college, they were always the prime suspects. It became obvious that Jonah and his college would be better off if they parted company. The parting of the ways happened at the end of the school year, at the beginning of the summer vacations.

Jonah's parents didn't know what to do with him. Schools in Mauritius were examination-oriented with a rigid academic curriculum. Students who didn't do well at the end of the secondary school examinations had very few options open to them. They were labelled as failures often for the rest of their life.

But Jonah's parents believed in him and were looking for ways and means to bring out the best in their son. But at the time he was sent away from school, they didn't know what to do with him.

THE DARE

Our story opens with Jonah hanging out with his friends, Gregory and Fabien, in the small coastal village of Albion where Jonah lives. They had climbed a steep slope to the top of the road when, out of the blue, Gregory came up with the dumbest idea he could come up with:

'Dude,' he dared Jonah, 'if you can go downhill on my little sister's *trottinette* (two-wheeled kick- scooter) I'll give you Rs 100.'

This slope is so dangerous that the kids in the neighbourhood call it *la descente de la mort* (death's slope). It is a 500 metre downhill drop on a road that is full of holes and strewn with small rocks. It is a slope that has claimed many casualties.

'Okay,' Jonah replied on an impulse.

Jonah had never been on a *trottinette* before. Even then he took up the challenge as he had not yet learnt to measure the risks involved.

When he took the scooter and looked down the slope, he felt sick and his heart sank, but instead of backing out of the dare, he jumped on the scooter and started the descent.

I shall now continue the story in Jonah's own words.

At the beginning everything was fine. I was doing more or less well, but as the scooter picked up speed and shot down the slope at breakneck speed I applied the brakes, but they didn't work! At the same time oncoming vehicles were whizzing past me like in some of my worst nightmares. I knew I was going to crash into a car if I did nothing.

102

Thoughts and images flashed through my mind. My heart was pumping hard, my mouth was dry and nauseous. I closed my eyes and jumped off the scooter. Halfway into the air I opened my eyes. Everything seemed to be happening in slow motion. I saw the ground approaching my head. I wrapped my arms around my head a nano second before I crash-landed. Then there was a heavy impact and I blacked out.

When I woke up, Fabien and Gregory were running towards me. I had landed on my left side. My left leg was bent and twisted from my pelvis all the way down to my ankle. Drops of blood were trickling down from my gashed lips. I tried to push myself up, using my arms. I could hear my bones crack as I tried to get up. My left elbow was hurting bad. It had been scraped raw with small rocks embedded into the wound through which a little bit of bone was showing.
'Shit! Gregory you idiot why did you get me into this!' I screamed knowing that I was the bigger idiot for accepting his challenge.

When I finally managed to stand up, I felt a sharp pain deep in my left pelvis, like something poking me from the inside. I fell back down.

'Guys, I'm badly hurt, I think I broke my pelvis!' I declared.

WARD G7

Entering Ward G7 was like entering hell: old haggard men tied to their beds; patients with their legs strung up in the air with weights and pulleys; a pervasive smell of fermented piss - an odour so horrible it made me want to jump off the yellow stained bed on which I was lying and crawl out of the ward. To cap it all, resident rats and cockroaches made sure you were kept awake with your eyes wide open.

'Well,' I told myself, 'looks like it's going to be a long stay.'

After an hour, a male nurse came towards me, he looked like an escaped inmate of some psychiatric asylum.

'Jonah Peerally,' he squeaked, 'the doctor has sent me to conduct some tests on you.'

'What kind of tests?' I asked a little nervous.

'Just the routine,' he said, while another nurse approached with a trolley bristling with my worst phobia - syringes and needles, of different lengths and sizes!

'Keep your arm straight boy,' he commanded in a voice that gave me the creeps.

He looked like a maniac. And he was smiling like the joker in Batman.

He grabbed my arm and asked the other nurse for a rubber tube. He wrapped the tube tightly around my arm. He took a syringe and told me to look away. He then proceeded to insert the syringe into my arm. I watched hypnotised as I saw the needle moving under the skin of my wrist while the nurse was looking for my vein like a vampire. After he found a thick blue vein, he chuckled with delight and drew out some blood, about a quarter of a pint. He then asked the other nurse for some cotton wool. He took a bigger and longer syringe. I cursed beneath my breath. He turned me on my belly and plunged the syringe into my buttocks.

He gave me about seven injections in all. After that he grinned wickedly and went away.

In the afternoon, my parents came to see me. Thank God they had brought my dinner and spared me the ordeal of eating the tasteless, smelly, disgusting hospital mix the nurses call food. When at dinner time I opened the small container of *briyani*, the delicious aroma wafted through the ward causing some patients to salivate into their smelly slop.

At night a nurse came and injected me with something that made me sleep.

The next day when I woke up, it was about five in the afternoon. The ward was as demoralizing as yesterday—if not more. This time we were treated to a volley of abuse by the nurses who were changing the patients' nappies. It was sickening to see sick people bullied like that. I was lucky my auntie was a nurse instructor at the hospital's Nurses' School. She came to see me every day and that certainly helped.

The nurses began to address me by my name and became on good terms with me. Even the doctor who was a friend of my auntie addressed me by my first name and kept my morale up.

After some more tests and X-rays, I was diagnosed with hip dislocation but fortunately there was no bone fracture. I was put on traction, and immobilised in bed with my left leg strung up with weights and pulleys.

At night after I had been injected with the sleep drug, I was woken up by one of the patients yelling 'Nurse! Nurse! Untie me! I have an important appointment.' The nurse shouted from across the ward.

'Shut up, you're disturbing the patients.'

"Untie me, I have a very important appointment.'

'What is it?' the nurse shouted back.

'I must meet the Prime Minister. Terrorists are planning to attack the airport!'

The old patient was delusional. The nurse cursed him and went back to sleep. I dozed off too. After an hour or two I was woken up again, this time all the patients were yelling for the nurse:

'Nurse! Nurse! Your patient is naked! He's running away! Stop him!' They were yelling at the top of their voices. The old man had freed himself and was running naked down the aisle towards the exit!

On day three I woke up to the sound of prayer. I opened my eyes and saw a Catholic priest bending over the patient on my right. The man was dying and the priest was administering *dernié sakreman* (extreme unction) to him a few minutes before he passed away. The body was retrieved later by relatives and another patient installed in his place.

On day four, I woke up again to the sound of prayer. I opened my eyes and my heart almost stopped when I saw the same priest bending over me, and looking into my eyes with great compassion.

For a crazy moment, I thought I had died and the good priest was administering *dernié sakreman* (extreme unction) to me to ease my transition to the other world. If I hadn't been immobilised, I would have leapt out of my bed and got the hell out of that madhouse.

The priest pressed my hand gently, smiled benignly and said,

'My child, you appear to be in bad shape. Would you like me to say a prayer for you. Prayers are a man's best medicine and have the power to comfort and heal.'

106

I felt so relieved I wasn't dead that I began to cry. I would have loved to have a priest pray for my quick recovery but I told him I was a Muslim and maybe that was not a good idea.

Before leaving me and attending to Amoy, the patient on my left, the priest said:

'My son, in the kingdom of God, there is no Jew, no Muslim, no Hindu, and no Christian. God is our father, and we are all his children.'

I found the nights very long and I was happy when the darkness outside began to break up a little and the soft light of dawn began to penetrate the darkness inside the ward. Every morning I strained my ears to catch the sounds and noises that announced the break of dawn and I felt better when the priest appeared and made his rounds. He always stopped for a minute or two beside my bed and asked me if I had slept well and how I was getting on.

There was one patient, about 68 years of age, who had been in the ward for about 18 months. His two sons, in their thirties, took turns to come every day early in the morning to clean and bathe him and make his bed, although the nurses were going to do that later. They brought newspapers and other things that he needed and made sure their old man was comfortable and well looked after.

There was one boy who lay immobilised in his bed for three years. He had a problem with his knee bones. He still hoped he would get better and would be able one day to walk.

And there were those whom nobody ever came to visit except the priest.

I had plenty of time to think. Maybe I should make an effort and keep out of trouble and not distress my poor mother who was overburdened with work both at home and in the office, and had not a minute to herself.

I felt that when I grew up I would like to engage in a work which would make me go out to people, to get to know them, to befriend them, to help them.
While I lay immobilised on my bed, I befriended Amoy, an old crippled Chinese man, who occupied the bed on my left. When he slept during the day he looked like a corpse. And when he woke up at night, he sang in Chinese. He did not speak any other language. So I taught him some Creole.

After seven days, the doctor came and inspected my leg. He concluded that it was time to take me off the weight treatment.
After they took the weights off, I was given the use of a wheelchair. But getting into the wheelchair was much more difficult than I had thought.
When I put my feet on the floor, they felt weird. And when I tried to stand up, my feet could not support my body. I had lost all sense of balance. I sat on my bed and tried again and again. This time I stood up and as soon as I felt myself falling, I threw my good leg and my body on the wheelchair.

As soon as I was in the wheelchair, I felt the first urge in seven days to go to the toilet. The nurses had wanted to fit me with a nappy, but I would have none of it. The result was I hadn't emptied my bowels for seven long days. Now I could feel the avalanche coming. I used the wheelchair like a racing car, and I wheeled it so fast I nearly knocked Mister Crazy Nurse off balance!

108

As I entered the toilet, a terrible stench assaulted my nostrils but I ignored it. I had hardly sat on the toilet seat when my long-suffering bowels started pushing towards the exit to empty themselves. But the passage was too tight and narrow. After labouring painfully for a few minutes, I finally felt I had shitted a wood log! It hurt so much the whole ward heard my screams!

When I got out, I felt ten times lighter and better. This was one time I had experienced nirvana, pure bliss!

For the first time in seven days, I was able to go outside and see the sky. There, I met Ashok, a trucker who broke his leg in four places when his truck ran over it as he was changing a tyre. He was smoking so I asked him if I could have a puff. After that I felt a new man.

As we had plenty of time and not much to do, those of us who were mobile often assembled on the veranda where we entertained each other with jokes and funny stories. There's one story that Ashok told us that I thought very funny.

I had told the story of a patient who had his wrong leg amputated.

'I want to tell you a real story,' Ashok said. 'It's about that man whose right foot was his left foot. So the doctor cut off a piece of his right foot to make it level with as his left foot. Unfortunately, the doctor cut off a bit too much, and this time his left foot was longer than his right foot! So the doctor cut off a piece of the left foot to make it level with the right foot. This time the right foot was a bit longer than the left foot. After two more operations the doctor got it right. Both the man's feet were of the same length. There was just one thing though. When the man had come to the hospital he was 5 feet 8. When he left the hospital he was 4 feet 4!'

Well as crazy as it may sound, I had got used to that wretched place. I believe I had actually grown fond of 'my' ward. I had even got used to its distinctive smells. I came to like the patients too, they were all very cool.

I think I had begun to enjoy my days at the hospital!

AMOY

I shall now take over from Jonah and tell the story from my perspective, from the perspective of the granddad who saw in Jonah a sensitive and an intelligent child who was going to the dogs.

When I visited Jonah, he was lying on his back, immobilised in his bed, with his left foot suspended in mid-air. On his left, an emaciated Chinese man lay with his eyes closed. He was very skinny and the bones on his shoulder and chest showed through his paper-thin skin and you could trace his skeleton through his pale yellow skin. He looked like a corpse.

Whenever I looked at him I felt a cold shiver run down my spine as if a goose had stepped over my grave.

Nobody visited him and nobody seemed to care about him.

The second day I visited Jonah, he couldn't move but I could see he was trying to communicate with the Chinese patient. As I approached, I could see him point at his face and say '*figir*'. Then he pointed at his head and said '*latet*'.

'What are you doing?' I asked.

'*Grandpa*,' Jonah said, 'this is Amoy. Amoy, this is my *grandpa*. *Grandpa*, say *bonzour* (good morning) to Amoy. Amoy speaks only Chinese. He doesn't know any other language. So I'm teaching him some Creole words to help him get by.'

When I visited Jonah on the 7th day after he had been taken off traction and could move, I saw him sitting on the side of Amoy's

110

bed. He was trying to get Amoy in a reclining position and make him drink some orange juice.

As soon as Jonah saw me, he said,

'*Grandpa*, can you hold Amoy's head for me, I want to make him drink a little juice and eat some food.'

In any other circumstances, I would have been eager to help, but I'm ashamed to say, the idea of touching Amoy was too much for me. I just wouldn't go near him, nor look at him, let alone touch him!

I mumbled some excuse.

'Jonah, you shouldn't mess with patients. You might make them worse.'

'No *grandpa*, see how thirsty he is. He hasn't been fed for the last few days. He wouldn't eat when the nurses tried to force-feed him. He wouldn't even drink a little juice. Look at his eyes. They are smiling. Look how much he's enjoying the food.' Then turning to Amoy he said, 'Amoy, that's okay for now. I'll give you some more later.'

One day, Jonah asked me to bring some 'special' fried noodles from one of the Chinese restaurants that made the best noodles in town.

When I brought the noodles to him for his lunch, he was very happy.

'*Grandpa*,' he told me, please help me prop up Amoy and hold his head straight while I feed him. Don't worry, Amoy eats very little. I'll finish the rest.'

I was about to mumble some excuses, but Jonah was fixing me with a no-nonsense look on his face. I did as I was told.

Amoy was very old, way past 80. When I supported his head on the pillow, he felt as light as a feather. Then I held him in my arms as one would hold a child. I was glad I had fought back my initial repugnance. I was grateful to Jonah for helping me overcome my fear and bringing out the goodness in me.

I tasted then the sweetness of service and the joy of caring for others.

The ward was an orthopaedic ward with patients with broken bones and multiple injuries. Some patients were in pain, a few were beyond pain. When I first visited the ward, it was a cheerless place made more dismal by the occasional screams of pain and delirious scraps of monologues addressed to nobody in particular.

Jonah and those of his friends who could walk or hobble on their crutches started going round the ward, making friends with the bedridden patients. They were careful not to disturb those who were more seriously injured.

Jonah and his friends often lounged on the veranda of the ward, where I suspected they shared a cigarette that they were careful to hide whenever somebody walked past.

On some of my visits, I saw Jonah on his bed, surrounded by some patients, talking, laughing and cracking jokes.

At other times, he would be sitting on the side of some patient's bed, surrounded by a group of friends.

After some time, even the nurses seemed to have changed. Before, I was grumpily allowed in to feed Jonah. Now as soon as they saw me, they rose from behind their table and greeted me cheerfully:

'Jonah, your grandpa has come to see you!'

The ward was gradually changing into a more hospitable place. It was the same ward, but something had changed. It was no

112

longer a cold and impersonal place. It seemed more relaxed and more cheerful. It had become a warm, welcoming home where sick persons were being looked after, cared for, until they were well enough to go home to their families.

I was there when Jonah was discharged from hospital. I had gone to pick him up and bring him back home. I helped him gather his few things in a bag.
I didn't see the joy that I had expected to see on his face, the joy of finally being released; something like the euphoria, for example, that I had felt after I had myself been discharged after spending twelve days at the Cardiac Centre, following an open heart surgery.

Jonah was slow in his movements, and in his speech.
I also noticed that the ward was unusually quiet. There was not the usual hum and buzz of activity and conversation.
After we had packed his few things in the bag, instead of rushing for the exit, Jonah asked me to please wait until he had said goodbye to his friends.
'Okay, Jonah, go ahead, take your time, there's no hurry.'
'Thank you *grandpa*,' he said.
Jonah then went to each and every patient in the ward. He stopped at each and every bed, held the patients' hands, clapped them on their backs, shook their hands, laughed, cried, and said goodbye.

Finally he stopped beside Amoy's bed.
He sat on the side of the bed, held Amoy's hands in his, spoke to him in Creole. Amoy shook his head, looked at him, his eyes filling with tears. When Jonah rose to go, Amoy pulled himself

113

up, and, folding his arms across his chest, he bowed his head in the Chinese gesture of affection and respect, and said something in Chinese.

It sounded to me like he was saying 'God bless you, Jonah. Come and see me.'

Jonah replied, 'Good bye, Amoy, my dear friend, and take good care of you. I will come and see you soon.'

And when he was about to leave the ward, he turned and said,

'*Au revoir, mes amis* (Good-bye, dear friends), you can count on me. I promise I will come and see you soon!'

When he climbed into the car, he again looked back at Ward G7. The tears that had been brimming in his eyes started to stream down his face.

***

DANCING IN THE RAIN

Life isn't about surviving storms. It's about dancing in the rain.

'We're off next week to Mumbai to attend a wedding. Why don't you join us?'
And that started it all. This casual invitation was floated by Shobha just when Meera and I were leaving after a delicious dinner at Rajen and Romy Subbamah's house one late Saturday evening.
'That's a great idea,' I quickly replied before Shobha could change her mind, 'count us in. By the way, who's getting married?'

Meera loved travelling and was always eager to get away in spite of the fact that, at the age of thirty-five, she'd suffered a stroke that had left her speech and physical movements severely impaired. Notwithstanding, in our younger days, I made it a point to take her with me whenever possible on overseas assignments, thus combining business with pleasure.
But after I had survived a heart bypass surgery at the age of sixty-eight, I was advised by my doctors that, because of my heart's erratic behaviour, I was not to engage in any strenuous or stressful activity, and to take special care of my health.
'You can live a normal life,' they cautioned, 'but everything in moderation, *mollo mollo* - no passion, no intensity, no stress, no strain.'
But that was more easily said than done.

We had practically no friends of our age left in Mauritius as most of them had long emigrated to 'greener pastures'.

But it so happened that through my eminently sociable younger brother-in-law, Chic, and his no less eminently vivacious wife, Shobha, we were admitted as honourable members of their jet-setting group of friends, all of whom aged between 40 and 50, practically about one generation younger than us.

Meera and myself participated fully in their exciting parties, outings, disputes, break-ups and reconciliations. I survived this fast-paced lifestyle but was finding it increasingly difficult to keep up with the group.

I knew I was getting on when the younger girls in the group started addressing me as 'uncle' and *'mamou'*, and giving me the attention normally bestowed on the elderly.

And when on late evenings one or two of the younger ladies sat on my lap, and hugged me and cuddled me as a prize pet, I was in no doubt as to my advanced senior citizen status in the group.

I even drew my friends' attention to my 'privileged' treatment, but no one took me seriously and laughed my comments off as a joke,

'You're safe,' Chic chuckled good-humouredly.

'Tu es inoffensif!' Rajen added for good measure, followed by giggles and guffaws.

If they were happy with that, who was I to disillusion them!

If travelling by air is a picnic for others, for us it was quite an adventure, with all the thrills and risks that it entails.

We were no longer as young as we wanted to believe, at least this is what our bodies kept reminding us.

116

I still remember once in Jomtien, 165 km from Bangkok, I had lost my bag containing my passport, tickets, money in foreign currency and travellers' cheques.

Being stranded in a Far Eastern country, at the mercy of the local police, without an Embassy to bail you out, was no joking matter. I'd heard of people arrested by the Police and never ever heard of again.

'It's worse than losing yourself,' a commiserating soul had remarked.

Just thinking about what could have happened to me still gives me goose bumps.

I also had a phobia about dying overseas. I knew that, like all mortals, I was condemned to die. But I wanted to die in my bed, with my family and close friends around me. Not alone in some faraway country with no one to hold my hands.

Meera and I were getting on *clopin-clopant* like a horse and carriage and our life was threatening to settle into a comfortable routine. And this was the last thing we wanted to happen to us.

To make matters worse, as many of our friends were cadres of Air Mauritius, our national airline, or otherwise associated with the travel and tourism industry, they were flying in and out all the time while we seemed to be stuck to the ground like land crabs.

Something had to be done. The trouble was we didn't trust ourselves to travel on our own. We didn't walk; we shuffled like old people do. We had difficulty climbing stairs and Meera was scared of escalators.

We thought of going on cruises. The idea of sitting on board while the ship did all the travelling was appealing. But we couldn't find the right package and kept deferring until all the conditions were right.

So when Shobha invited us to join the wedding party, we readily agreed. Within one week all the arrangements had been made and travel formalities completed: visas, air tickets, hotel accommodation at special wedding-party rates, transfers to and from the hotel.

But there was one hitch. Our return tickets could not be confirmed as the flights from Mumbai for the whole month was completely booked out.

To go or not to go, that was now the question. To sit tight in our comfort zone or to venture out boldly. I still remembered once we had been stranded in Mumbai for a whole month, and had it not been for the intervention of a friend's friend at the Air India Mumbai office, we would have been waiting forever. To add insult to injury, when we finally got on the plane, we found it was half empty!

We had been through some rough patches before but it had always turned out right in the end.

What the hell, let's go, I finally decided. We'll cross the bridge when we come to it.

Life, after all, isn't about surviving storms. It's about dancing in the rain!

Attending a wedding overseas has everything to commend it especially to an ageing couple.

It means breaking out of our routine, recapturing the thrills and excitement of our youthful days while travelling in comfort and in the company of relatives and close friends.

118

It also means there's a focus to our 'vacation'; and entertainment guaranteed for at least three to four consecutive nights, not to mention the satisfaction that a sizeable number of 'home' guests procures to the bride/groom and their parents.

As a matter of fact, inter-country wedding is setting a new trend with the modern generation. The world is getting global including marriage partners. People from different countries and cultures meet during holidays, at the university, at work, fall in love and get married, either in the boy's home country or in the girl's, or. in some romantic or exotic destination of their choice.

Attending weddings in a different country could well become a preferred way of spending one's holidays, just like attending conferences or rallies.

It has everything: a focus, thrills, conviviality, loads of fun, entertainment *ā gogo*! One could just as well plan one's holidays around an away-wedding.

CELEBRATIONS

The groom was a nephew of Shobha's. He worked in a bank in New York and the bride was a colleague of his. She was Indian by birth and the wedding was to take place in Mumbai, not far from Mangalore where the bride's parents resided.

The wedding, like most modern Indian weddings, was a three-day affair: *sangeet, mehendi & haldi*, and the *vivaah samskar* (wedding ceremony) proper, preceded by a Welcome Reception. Our five-day stay flew past like a roller-coaster ride.

Since I had embarked on the trip with a vacation mindset and not as a wedding guest, I thought I could get away with dressing smart casual. That dispensed me from dressing formal or Indian traditional. Meera wasn't happy. As a compromise, I decided to pack my suit and wear it for all the occasions when one was

119

expected to dress formal or traditional. It reminded me of my student days when I wore my one-and-only suit as an all-purpose uniform: for parties and college functions, for weddings and funerals, for visits and interviews.

DAY ONE: WELCOME RECEPTION

On day one itself, after checking in at the hotel and a short rest, we sallied forth to Colaba, where each went about their own business - some looking for eyeglasses, filigree jewellery - necklaces, matching bracelets and earrings; others for crystals and semi-precious stones; while others hunted for shoes, sandals and other specific items like saffron and tongue-scrapers that they don't get in Mauritius. After lunch at *Leopold's*, we rushed back to the hotel for a short rest.

The Welcome Reception in the evening at the *Tote on the Turf*, a rather unique location within the *Mahalaxmi Racecourse*, turned out to be a glitzy and glam affair where all the guests, men and women, Indian and Mauritian, had dressed out in tuxedos and Indian traditional. The women, Western and Indian alike, were flaunting the latest Mumbai fashions and converted the function into a glamorous Bollywood film sequence. On the other evening celebrations, all the 'western' guests wore Indian traditional outfits down to peaked Aladdin-like sandals.

Boy was I glad I had brought my all-purpose suit with me in my suitcase!

My one-and-only suit and tie had allowed me to show respect for the occasion, to honour the groom's parents, and had spared me the embarrassment of feeling like a fish out of water

First thing the next day, I bought three silk hand-embroidered *kurtas* and matching shawls to wear for the other celebrations.

120

When I arrived at the reception, the first thing I wanted to do was find out who the bridegroom was. After all, I was 'crashing' his party. At the bar, I met this impeccably dressed young man, and, after exchanging salutations, I told him about my predicament and asked him, *sotto voce*, if he could spot the bridegroom out for me.

'I'm so sorry I didn't introduce myself,' he chuckled. 'I'm Dhanny Mundil. My friends call me Tish. I'm actually the bridegroom. I'm delighted you and Meera could make it. I've been looking forward to thanking you personally.'

DAY TWO: *SANGEET* (MUSIC) NIGHT

The girls in our group were all seasoned travellers and knew exactly what they wanted and where to get them. On the morning of the second day, they sallied forth to their preferred boutiques and stores to purchase the latest in sarees, *lehenga cholis*, *salwar kameez, anarkalis* and other stylish varieties of Indian wear. I watched fascinated by the shopping frenzy that had gripped them. They sifted through scores of dresses, tried them on, had them altered, adjusted and delivered at their hotel that same evening, prior to being driven out to the *Tote on the Turf*, where the *Sangeet* (Music) Night was to take place.

Rajen Subbamah, who had also joined the wedding group with his wife Romy, also got caught up in the shopping frenzy that had gripped everybody. Rajen has the face of Govinda on a Salman Khan body that he adores dressing up. Every costume he was trying on looked as if it had been tailor-made for him. He bought four full-length princely costumes including two *sherwanis* in a designer boutique at fixed prices.

'Ramesh,' he kept urging me, 'have you any idea how much this costume costs in Mauritius? Not less than 25,000 Mauritian Rupees. Here it costs 25,000 Indian Rupees, equivalent to 12,500 Mauritian Rupees. I'm buying four of them at 100,000 Indian Rupees, equivalent to 50,000 Mauritian Rupees.

'Actually, I'm not spending Rs 100,000. I'm saving Rs 50,000!'

He used the same disconcerting logic to buy four pairs of shoes and kept urging me to make the most of the bonanza. If he had more time, he would have bought sunglasses, shirts, scarves, belts and loads of other luxury items.

That evening, we were entertained by solo and group performances on both the bride's and bridegroom's parties. The Mauritian party put on a lively group Bhojpuri dance with 100 % audience participation that brought the house down. I don't have to say it, but my chest expanded like an ironsmith's bellows, fired as it was at the sight of ten of our beautiful girls, a few of them beauty contestants and beauty queens in their younger days. They were joined onstage by the groom's parents.

They did their country proud. And Bihar also, from where most Mauritian immigrants originate.

The American and British male friends of the bride and groom performed an uproarious native *lungi* dance that threatened to become a belly-aching striptease show!

After the show, young and not-so-young alike got on the dance floor and tried to break it down incited by a mix of Indian and American remixes. What's great about Indian dancing is you don't have to dance as long as you hold your hands in the air and sway your hips back and forth and side to side. We were dragged onto the dance floor in spite of my huffing-and-puffing like some world-war-one steam engine. But believe it or not, despite the aches and the cramps, we were actually having the time of our life although my doctors would have thrown up their hands in despair if they had seen us.

DAY THREE: *MEHENDI* & *HALDI* CEREMONY

A *mehendi* expert was at hand to apply *mehendi* (henna designs) on the bride's hands, arms, feet and legs. She went on to apply *mehendi* on the hands and arms of all the ladies in the group. The effect was disconcerting: same ladies, different women!

This was followed by the *Haldi* ceremony when turmeric paste (made from turmeric, rosewater, sandalwood powder and other fragrant ingredients) is applied to both the bride's and groom's face, feet and hands by their relatives and friends accompanied by traditional Haldi songs. This could not be done with recorded music, as the words of the songs have to be in synch with the rituals taking place.

Here again, our girls did us proud.

Haldi songs are nostalgic songs, hallowed by tradition and the memory of our great grandmothers who had sung the same songs at the *haldi* of their children and passed them on from generation to generation. And here, for the first time, I was hearing the same songs sung by their 21st century descendants, dressed not in humble *hornis* and *lehengas*, but in fashionable *sarees, anarkalis, salwar kameez.* The ceremony was taking place not in some lowly thatched hut in an obscure village, but in a decor fit for kings and queens.

Day Four: Wedding Ceremony

I had the impression I was watching a Bollywood movie.

All the rites and rituals and celebrations had gone off smoothly with due regard to tradition and modernity, and, where appropriate, lavishly accompanied with snacks, appetisers, great-tasting food, desserts and *mithai* (sweets), and a non-stop supply of alcoholic and non-alcoholic drinks,

After the second day, however, I couldn't touch Indian food and opted for clear soup and mineral water instead.

DAY FIVE: ALL OUT SHOPPING

After we had come back from our shopping forays to well-known up-market boutiques, one of our lady friends excitedly announced she had discovered a treasure trove in the mall adjoining our hotel. Although we could hardly stand on our feet, Meera and I once again tagged along as best we could to what turned out to be a veritable shopping Eldorado!
It was the end-of-January sales with 3O %, 50% and up to 70% discount.
To give you an idea, let's take an article that costs Rs 3,000 in Mauritius. At the store it was pegged at 3,000 Indian Rupees. With 50% discount it cost 1.500 Indian Rupees. Which is equivalent to 750 Mauritian Rupees!
The girls went berserk!
As far as I was concerned, I was only too happy I could still stand on my feet and feel part of the group. To be encumbered with luggage was the last thing I wanted.
By now we felt as if we had lead in our feet. We did not walk, we hobbled and shuffled about the mall like zombies!

And when the girls discovered that even brand names were selling at half their usual price, all of them, including Meera, wouldn't stop until it was time to get back to the hotel, get
124

dressed to receive friends who had come to visit, retire early and prepare for our pre-dawn departure flight.

The only jarring note was struck by Malcolm, our NRI friend who had come to visit. 'These sales actually are not seasonal,' he quipped, 'they are all-year-round seasonal sales!'

DAY SIX: DEPARTURE FOR MAURITIUS

With the exception of Rajen and Romy, none of us had confirmed tickets.

Our friends in Mumbai and Mauritius were moving heaven and earth to get all of us on board. But the plane was fully booked. The flights for the whole month were also fully booked out.

We therefore set out early for the airport to try our luck. There were always confirmed passengers who didn't show up. There were also a few crew seats that could be allocated to travelling staff.

'Not to worry,' the voice of my heart kept telling me. 'Things will turn out right.'

Our friends had agreed among themselves and the Air Mauritius authorities that because of our age and health status we would be given top priority. But of course there was no guarantee.

Once inside the enormous airport, the girls pressed on ahead and we hobbled behind. The terminal was bigger than a football stadium and stretched endlessly in every direction.

'Pa trakasé twa, nek swiv nou deryer (don't you worry, just follow our derrière (backside),' Shobha reassured me.

And this is what I did. I was so scared of getting left behind that I followed the girls and kept my eyes glued to their derrières.

I had seen them hundreds of times, but I had never noticed them before. It is as if I was seeing them for the first time. Each pair of derrières had their own distinctive behaviour and characteristics, especially the way they kept pitching and rolling,

125

bobbing and bumping against each other when in motion. One pair looked like two mongooses fighting in a sack. Another pair was more demure and jerked rhythmically like those of a model on a catwalk. I knew for certain which pair belonged to whom *(mo ti kapav rekonet sakenn par zot deryer)*!

When all the avenues to get all the odds in our favour had been explored, there was no option but to wait until all confirmed passengers had been checked in. So we left our suitcases in the care of an Air Mauritius official and we waited and waited, seated back to back on a row of benches somewhere towards the back of that enormous complex.

I wanted to go to the toilets, but preferred to wait.

After some time Meera felt she had to go to the toilets and shuffled off in the direction of the sign pointing to the facility.

Meera was taking a long time. Any moment now we could be called to check in.

I went to look for her. When I reached the toilets, she was coming out.

As I was already there, I decided I might as well relieve myself and told her to hurry and rally the group. I would join them in a few minutes.

When I came out of the toilets, I could not be sure whether to turn right or left. I turned in the direction I thought I had come. I rounded a corner and surveyed the vast expanse in front of me. I could not spot the benches where my friends had been waiting. I knew we had stationed ourselves within sight of the Air Mauritius check-in counters. I tried to get my bearings but could hardly make out the MK counters. I hobbled in the direction of some counters at the far side of the terminal. When I

126

approached, I saw they were the check-in counters of another airline.

I could feel the panic in the pit of my stomach rising and threatening to overpower me.
Don't panic, keep cool, everything will turn out fine in the end, I kept repeating like a mantra. But the panic attack was more powerful than anything I had ever experienced in my life.
I hobbled in the opposite direction as best I could. I rounded the corner and scanned the terminal. This time I could spot the benches where my friends had been waiting. But they were empty.
My heart began to pound heavily against my ribs.
Had they all rushed off to check in thinking I would join them later at the MK counters? What about Meera? I was sure she would have stayed behind and waited for me. Had she come looking for me and lost her way?
I tried to fight back the nausea that was engulfing me.
Then something happened. There was a quick succession of blinking lights. I could not focus, things were getting blurred and were swimming away before my eyes. My mind seemed to be shutting down. At the same time my feet were slipping from under me. I closed my eyes and tried to steady myself.
When I opened my eyes I felt strange. I was still in that cavernous place but something had changed.
On one side, the terminal seemed to stretch back into long dark recesses; On the other side I was looking down a long corridor which seemed to become progressively narrower and brighter.

I made my way towards the light, worrying about Meera, anguished that she might have been left behind.

I kept moving towards the light and noticed that my feet were no longer hurting. As a matter of fact, I was feeling lighter and better. I also noticed that the vast terminal was getting smaller and narrower, more like a tunnel than a hall. When I was about to emerge from the tunnel into the light, I could see a few metres away, a small group of people who were talking and laughing animatedly. They could not see me. I was still inside the tunnel.

I could even recognise their voices and make out who they were.

They were the voices and faces of loved ones who had departed the world, some recently, others a few years back.

I understood it was some kind of a reception party. Everybody I had known had turned up to welcome me: my father, mother, brothers and sisters, dear relatives, close friends, people I had loved as a child, as a teen and as an adult. They looked younger than they were when they had departed the world. I felt happy and eager to meet them.

I intuitively knew that the moment I stepped out into the light, I wouldn't be able to go back. I was about to emerge into the light, when a scream resonated along the depths of that long tunnel turning my blood to ice. I froze, turned and looked back. Far away in the recesses, I could see Meera's silhouette, crouching on the floor, wailing and screaming disconsolately.

I was overwhelmed with sadness and couldn't bear the thought of abandoning her when she needed me most.

I took a long lingering look at my loved departed ones, turned and hurried back in the direction of Meera's voice.

Next thing I knew, Meera was helping me to my feet. I told her I had slipped and fallen.

128

'We must hurry up,' she told me with tears streaming down her face. 'When I left the toilets and went back to join the group, we were told there were six no-shows and we could all be accommodated. Everybody hurried to check in and complete formalities for embarkation. I was trying to find you and join them later at the MK check-in counter.'

We made it to the plane just when they were about to close the gate. What is more, in order to release seats in Economy Class, Meera and I were upgraded to Business Class!

I've always said that the best thing about going away is coming back.
And once again, like many times in my life before, things had turned out fine in the end!
Soon we would be flying home!
On that special flight, home sounded like a magical word - a whole dimension of being and living, of loving, caring and belonging.
I told myself I have so much to be grateful for.
For five days, I had lived some of the most hectic moments of my life and some of the most traumatising as well.
I told myself, not only I had been gifted a bonus of years to live, but that after my experience at the airport, I should be counting my blessings every day for the rest of my life.

***

A NEW BEGINNING

AN OUT OF THE WORLD ADVENTURE

'When I consider Thy Heavens, the work of Thy fingers, the moon and the stars, which Thou hast ordained, what is man, that Thou art mindful of him?' Eighth Psalm

In the year 2112, Planet Earth had been devastated by a terrible war that had been waiting to happen. On the one hand, the more technologically advanced nations of the world had plundered the Earth's resources beyond the point of no return. Vital energy resources had become so scarce that the militarily powerful nations were using the flimsiest excuses to invade and appropriate the resources of less developed nations. On the other hand, religious radicalism and intolerance had made confrontation on a global scale inevitable.

In an ultimate attempt to save the human race from total extinction, the best scientific and creative brains in the world had been sent to outer space on board the 'Discovery', a specially designed spacecraft. I was fortunate to form part of these selected few. Our mission was to explore space, find other planets fit for human habitation, or with resources that could help sustain life on earth. We were scheduled to return in about 25 years, around the year 2187. By that time, the lethal gases unleashed in the global confrontation would have dissipated and the earth would have become once more fit for human habitation.

During the intervening period of 25 years, all of us on board the 'Discovery' would remain unaffected by the passage of time on

earth and we would come back without any perceptible change in our physical and physiological makeup.

We had been travelling for an indefinite number of years through time and space when a meteor smashed into our lateral rotors causing the 'Discovery' to spin out of control. After drifting helplessly for what seemed an eternity in an infinite ocean of space, our ship entered the atmosphere of an uncharted planet, and in less than no time, we found ourselves sucked at an incredible speed by its magnetic pull. It was clear that unless we slowed down and stabilized our ship, she would burn up and disintegrate under the forces of the planet's gravity. And even if she did not disintegrate, no one was going to survive the violence of the impact.

When it became clear that the end was near, all of us, each one in their own way, prepared to die. Some went down on their knees, others squatted on their haunches, a few spread themselves full-length in the aisles, invoking the name or the form of 'God' that was familiar to them. Even those who did not believe in the existence of God joined in the chants and prayers that reverberated throughout the length and breadth of the spaceship.

As for me, as is my wont, I began an interior dialogue with 'God'. As a matter of fact, I often 'talk' to Him. He is my closest confidant and I often refer to Him problems whose solution eludes me. This habit has often landed me in the soup. One night at a party, I had one too many and got engrossed in an animated conversation with Him. My friends were alarmed. They thought I had gone off my rocker. I therefore became more careful and talked to 'God' only when I was strictly alone. Even then, quite a few people thought I was weird and 'religiously' avoided me.

This time around, since I was faced with the prospect of imminent death, I reckoned that if God really did exist, He was surely going to respond to my lifelong queries. I therefore bared my soul to Him with single-minded earnestness.

'Lord,' I told Him, 'I'm not afraid to die, but how very sad that I should depart life before finding answers to the questions that have always bewildered me. You know how hard I've tried to search for the meaning of my life and the purpose of human existence. I have looked for answers in the sacred books of all the great religions of the world, and at the feet of renowned masters. I have implored you in my prayers to enlighten me about Man, God and the Universe. And now that I am about to die, I beseech you to take me into your confidence and respond to my heartfelt prayers. After a lifetime of one-way communication with you, I have grown more confused than ever. What a pity, Lord, if I should depart life as ignorant and as blind as when I first came into it! If I don't get any answers now, I will have no option but to conclude that you do not exist, and that I, along with millions of others, have only been fooling ourselves.'

Just then, as if in answer to our combined prayers and supplications, the spaceship began to steady herself. The pilot immediately took over the controls and managed to make a safe landing on a fairly flat surface of this mysterious planet. Within minutes, an advance party of armed scouts, of which I was a member, was sent out to reconnoitre the area within a 3-kilometre perimeter of our landing place.

132

We were advancing on a terrain that was not totally unfamiliar to me. It was strewn with rocks and boulders, and interspersed for as far as the eyes could see, with scrub and thickets. As we progressed further from the spaceship, I noticed that the terrain was getting bleaker and the atmosphere more and more stifling. When we lost sight of our ship altogether, the environment seemed to become even more inhospitable and oppressive. I thought I could discern shapes shifting in the shadows beyond.

'There's something moving over there,' I signalled to the others. 'Listen. Can you hear it. Sounds like something big!'

For some moments, everything lay as if suspended, in anticipation, in apprehension. I could hear my heart pounding uncontrollably against my ribs as fear began to engulf my whole being. Simultaneously, the noises in the undergrowth grew louder and more distinct.

We froze in our tracks, our fingers on the trigger, ready to open fire at sight. We could sense the presence of predators, prowling in the shadows, waiting for the moment to pounce on us. As our fear grew more uncontrollable, the light began to drain out of the place, and darkness began to settle in. We were by now thoroughly distraught and terrified. This is when, suddenly, our invisible enemies erupted from the thickets hemming us and attacked.

The creature that was charging me was no other than the monstrous Minotaur of my childhood nightmares. He was huge, with the powerful body of a man and the massive head and shoulders of a bull. I had read about the Minotaur when I was 11, and often dreamt I had lost my way in a labyrinth inhabited by the monster. This was the very creature that as a child I feared most.

I turned and ran in the direction of our spaceship. From the corner of my eyes I could see my teammates running for their lives too. An enormous, black, eight-legged, hairy spider had almost caught up with Ron. Black screeching birds with steel-grey beaks and vicious talons were attacking Aileen's face and eyes. Zimenez was only steps ahead of a viscous green horror with writhing snake-like tentacles. A monstrous gray rat had caught up with Benazir and had buried its crooked yellow teeth in her back.

The Minotaur was gaining on me. I could hear it bellowing balefully, its hot breath on the back of my neck. I prayed with all my heart and soul that this whole thing was not real, that soon I was going to wake up and find that it had all been a nightmare. As the demonic creature bore down on me, goring my buttocks with its ferocious horns, I was catapulted several feet in the air and blacked out.

When I regained consciousness, and found I was still alive, I thought that I had awakened from a nightmare. But when I looked at the desolate landscape around me and felt the pain in my backside, I knew I was not hallucinating. I got painfully back on my feet and made my way to where I thought our spaceship had landed. But there was no sign of the Discovery, nor of any other human being. The mission Commander must have given us up for lost and left in a hurry, judging the planet far too dangerous for human settlement. In which case, I was marooned, perhaps for life, on this strange planet.

I began to think of my family and my home before the man-made apocalypse took away everything I loved in this life. Even then, I realized I still wanted to return to planet Earth. That pale blue dot suspended in the vastness of the universe was still

134

home to me. It was the place where I was born, and it had held all the life and all the things I knew and loved. And to me, it was still the most beautiful place in the whole universe.

A sharp pain in my back brought me back to reality. I started to look, as best I could, for a place where I could find shelter and be able to nurse my wounds before I grew too weak. This is when I began to notice perceptible changes in the environment. The terrain which had at first appeared bleak and forbidding was changing before my very eyes. Instead of scrub and boulders, I could see bushes and trees sprouting all over the place. Soon I found myself in a forest full of exotic plants, wild flowers, giant ferns and tall trees overhung with creepers.

'Is this the garden of Eden?' I asked myself. 'Am I dead and wakened up in Paradise?'

The place reminded me of the virgin Amazonian rainforests that I had often seen in documentaries and Hollywood films. It immediately occurred to me that the Amazonian rainforests are inhabited by wild animals, and its rivers teem with ferocious piranhas and fearsome anacondas. No sooner had these thoughts entered my mind than the luxuriant forest began to assume a wild and threatening aspect.

'Why fear when Thou art near,' I said, repeating the phrase to myself like a mantra, 'why fear when Thou art near.'

As I prayed, the dense rainforest began to shed its wild aspect and looked more like a vast natural garden. The harder I prayed, the safer I felt until I realized like a certainty that I need not be afraid as long as I had faith, that the only thing I needed to fear was fear itself.

I was very hungry and thirsty. How wonderful if I could find something to eat and drink. No sooner had the thought entered my head than I noticed the branches of the trees bending under the weight of a great variety of fruits, and heard the gurgling of a stream among the flowering bushes and fruit-laden trees. I ate my fill of those delicious fruits and splashed happily like a child in the crystal-clear water of the stream.

When I lay down beside the stream, I found, much to my amazement, that the bruises and lacerations inflicted on my buttocks had completely healed. It was all too wonderful to be true. I decided that I had to take stock of the situation and find some explanation before proceeding to explore the planet further.

First of all, I reassured myself that I was alive and fully awake. I began to go over all my experiences ever since our spaceship had entered the atmosphere of this mysterious planet. It was strange but true that whenever I had wished ardently for something, my desires had been instantly fulfilled. And my fears also. Since the beginning of our mission, I had been secretly afraid of being cast adrift in outer space. And 'coincidentally' this is what happened. After the meteor smashed into our ship, we were all doomed. 'Coincidentally' our combined prayers had saved all of us from certain death. It was weird but how come I had been chased by my worst childhood phobia? The Minotaur of my childhood nightmares had not left me altogether. It had been buried deep within my subconscious and had been actualised by my fears. Similarly, Ron had been pursued by a giant spider, the bogey he most feared. Aileen, likewise, was inordinately scared of birds ever since she had seen Alfred Hitchcock's 'The Birds'! Benazir was, likewise, insanely scared of rats! Our fears had taken a physical form and had turned against us!

'If you run away from your fears,' a voice within me was saying, 'your fears will chase you. Always face what you fear, and it will go away!'

I decided it was very important for me to test this hypothesis before proceeding further. I therefore summoned from the depths of my subconscious my phobia of the Minotaur. And as I had anticipated, the terrifying creature appeared and charged me. This time I didn't turn and run. Instead, I held my ground. When it was about ten feet from me, I willed the creature to get lost and disappear forever. The Minotaur stopped in its tracks, looking undecided, moving its massive head from side to side. For a few moments it stood there, looking more and more like a mechanical toy. Then with a squeaking bellow, it disintegrated and vanished into thin air.

After this, I was convinced that I didn't have anything to fear except fear itself. I decided then that the first thing that I should do was to overcome my fears and think only of positive, wholesome and life-enhancing things. Every time a dark thought crossed my mind, I noticed that the environment began to change for the worse. I therefore quickly erased, so to say, all the negative associations as they arose.

Immediately I felt lighter, more relaxed, as if I had been rid of a heavy burden. The environment also became more attractive, the colours brighter, the light clearer. I forced myself to remain motionless, to listen to the sounds of nature and absorb the peace around me. Gradually I became very calm and began to feel in complete harmony with everything around me. I felt I was not a separate entity but as much part of the natural environment as a tree, a flower, a river, a mountain. I started to feel one with the universe.

As I felt more and more connected to the web of life, I discovered reservoirs of power and potential in me that I had never suspected before. I could walk for hours without feeling in the least tired or exhausted. I could cross rivers by tripping lightly over rock and water. I felt I could calm the waves, command the winds, heal the sick, inspire multitudes, if I felt like it. In truth I found I could make things happen simply by the force of my will.

I had the feeling that within a relatively short time, I had achieved a state of empowerment that it took sages on earth many years and even many lifetimes to achieve. I was discovering a treasure within me that I had been seeking all my life without knowing what it was I was seeking.

But more than the powers that had been conferred on me, I wished to acquire the knowledge and wisdom that would enable me to find answers to the questions that had always bewildered me.

Does God exist? Where has the Universe come from? Who or what has caused it? What is the place and role of man in this universal drama?

As this desire grew more and more intense, I felt transported to the foothills of a towering mountain whose summit was shrouded in clouds. It could have been Mount Kailash or Mount Olympus or any of the mountains that man has held sacred. I started to climb the mountain until I came across a stream. I sat down beside the stream and sank myself in deep meditation. I don't know how long I remained in this state, but it seemed to me that knowledge enormous like summer showers came pouring upon me and soak my being through and through. I felt elevated to a higher level of consciousness, and could see into the life of things.

I woke up in a place filled with light. Some distance away, I could see the Buddha. He was surrounded by countless Buddhas and other self-realized souls. He had a most kind and loving face, free of passion and attachment, yet filled with compassion for one and all.

I beheld a long line of Prophets, most of whom were unknown to me, but I could recognize Noah, Moses, Abraham and a few others. And then, even before I willed it, I beheld Jesus. He looked different from what he is generally portrayed on earth. He was tall, dark with a leathery complexion and a salt and pepper beard. He was talking to his disciples. His face was suffused with love and compassion. Some distance away I beheld an austere presence and knew at once that it was the Prophet Muhammad.

I was overcome with awe, wonder, joy and happiness.

As I strolled down the mountain slopes, trying to make sense of all that I had seen and experienced so far, I started to reflect upon some of the rituals and modes of worship that were prevalent in many parts of the world but which many people of other faiths considered bizarre and superstitious.

While I was lost in my musings, the place had undergone a total transformation. I found myself in a landscape which looked very much like what I imagined ancient India looked like. I beheld Shiva and Parvati with their sons, Ganesha and Kartikeya. I beheld Ram, Sita and Luchmun in their forest hermitage. In a clearing, Krishna was playing the flute and the *gopis* (milkmaids) were dancing to his melodious strains. I beheld many of the deities venerated by man enacting scenes that are dear to their devotees.

I always had some difficulty reconciling all these different lores and beliefs and draw the line between myth, legend, religion and spirituality. Suddenly in this place, I had no difficulty seeing the unity behind the diversity of forms, names and manifestations.

'God is both one and many at the same time. The manifest is many and the unmanifest is one,' a Voice was saying. 'From the beginning of time, Man has sought to understand the mysteries of life and his own place in the universe. Who am I? What am I doing here? How do I relate with the rest of creation? He has adored God in different ages, in different parts of the world, according to the customs and traditions prevailing in different cultures and civilisations. There are those who worship a formless God. There are many, though, who give Him a form and a name and worship Him in this way. To have a personal relationship with an embodiment of the divine is a profoundly transforming experience that brings the seeker closer to the transcendental and universal God. God's love, to be sure, is so great and all-embracing that He comes to his devotees in the form they love most.'

The words of a great sage I admired echoed in my ears:
'As the different streams having their sources in different places all mingle their waters in the sea, so the different paths which

men take through different tendencies, various though they appear, crooked or straight, all lead to Thee.'

'A person who realizes this truth,' the Voice continued, 'will never condemn the religion of others, or ridicule the rites and ceremonies through which others seek to meditate upon the Divine.'

When the Voice finished speaking, a blue light touched me and I found myself back in the foothills of the mountain. In the distance, I saw the Discovery being readied for immediate take-off. I sat down and sank deep in reflection. After my initial scare, this mysterious planet had not only fulfilled all my desires, it had also blessed me with knowledge that was far beyond all the riches of the world. On this planet I had at last found absolute peace and happiness. Why should I leave and resume a life so full of uncertainties and unhappiness? I could stay here and remain in this blessed state forever.

But a voice deep within told me that my place was with my fellow human beings. After all, I was born on planet Earth among human beings. That was still my home. It was the place in which all the people that had ever meant anything to me had lived and died. It was a pity that delusions of grandeur, greed and ignorance had turned us against one another. And yet we had been capable of amazing things. I should go back and in my own way try and help the human race in their heroic but often misguided efforts to find peace and happiness.

I shouted and signalled to the crewmen to wait for me. But they were far away and could neither see nor hear me. I closed my eyes and wished with all my heart and soul to be homeward bound on board the Discovery. When I opened my eyes, I found myself on board the ship, being warmly welcomed by everybody on board.

I learnt later that all the other members of the advance party had managed to escape their pursuers, and had made it safely to the ship. I was the only one missing. Armed parties had been sent out to find me. After they had given up all hope of finding me, and were about to leave, there I was, appearing as if from nowhere!

As the Discovery blasted off on our return journey to Earth, I was all too aware of the enormous responsibility that rested on my shoulders. I prayed with all my heart and soul to be a worthy instrument of the Divine Will. And help mankind make a new beginning.

***

ABOUT THE AUTHOR

Mauritian educationist, poet, novelist and short story writer, Ramdoyal's writings comprise a range of texts in English and Mauritian Creole, all of which bring out his main concern: Mauritius and its distinctive pluricultural society.

Born on March 28, 1939, in Rivière du Rempart, Ramdoyal spent the earlier part of his childhood in his native village. When his family moved to the city of Port-Louis, Ramdoyal found himself evolving amidst a vibrant pluricultural community in the foothills of Signal Mountain. Exposure to these two different worlds at a very young age became one of the sources of inspiration for his writings as the island, though small, is striking in its juxtaposition of cultures and lifestyles.

At the end of his secondary schooling at the Royal College of Port-Louis, he became a laureate of *La Bourse d'Angleterre* in 1958. This enabled him to go overseas to study English Language and English Literature in Dublin, and subsequently in Oxford. He went on later to the University of London, where he received his Master of Philosophy in Education.

In the meantime, Ramdoyal developed a keen interest in the socio-economic development of his homeland. On his return to the island in 1971, he served as Private Secretary to Sir Seewoosagur Ramgoolam, the first Prime Minister of Mauritius. Given his interest in education, he became one of the pioneers of the Mauritius Institute of Education (MIE), where he served as Director from 1980 to 1997.

By then, Ramdoyal became widely known not only as the author of *The Development of Education* in Mauritius (1977), but also for his collection of stories in *Tales from Mauritius (1979), More Tales from Mauritius (1981), Further Tales from Mauritius (2012)*. His interest in his mother tongue emerged in two of his works: a set of poems entitled *La Mare Mo Mémoire* (1985) and *The Prisoner of Conscience* (1990), an English translation of the award-winning play *Li*. He produced another work, *Festivals of Mauritius*, in 1990. This was designed as an introduction to the island's multi-religious heritage, and a French translation, *Maurice ă Travers Ses Fêtes*, was published the following year.

In 2014, Ramdoyal published a collection of poems in English entitled *The Islander's Song & Other Poems*. His biographical fiction *An Islander's Journey* and two more books in Mauritian Creole are awaiting publication..

Ramdoyal currently lives in Quatre Bornes, Mauritius, and continues to write in his spare time. He hopes to continue contributing to local and international literature in the years to come.

Also by Ramesh Ramdoyal
Tales From Mauritius
More Tales From Mauritius
Further Tales From Mauritius published by Osman Publishing
The Islander's Song - A Collection of Poems
An Islander's Journey - The Adventures of Robin Rai published by the President's Fund For Creative Writing.

Printed in Great Britain
by Amazon